"Invite me in, Mia."

And then his lips were on hers again, taking her in another mind-numbing kiss. Her soul was seared, branded by a man she hardly knew. Yet it felt right. So very right. How could she be so attracted to the same man her sister had slept with? Conceived a baby with? This wasn't going to happen. It couldn't.

Her little plan was backfiring.

Because as much as the battle raged inside her head with all those thoughts, she couldn't stop kissing Adam. She couldn't stop wanting him. She hadn't yet said yes or no and his kisses kept coming, delving and probing her mouth, his lips teasing and tempting hers. A strangled sound rose from her throat. "Adam."

She was breathless, out of oxygen and falling fast.

He was an amazing kisser.

He was probably an amazing lover.

How long had it been since she'd been flipped inside out like this?

Maybe never.

She slipped a hand into her beaded purse, grabbed for her key and pressed it into his hand. "You're invited in," she said, her voice a raspy whisper.

* * *

The Billionaire's Daddy Test
is part of Harlequin Desire's #1 bestselling series,
Billionaires and Babies: Powerful men...wrapped
around their babies' little fingers.

Dear Reader,

The Billionaire's Daddy Test combines two of my favorite things in the world: adorable if feisty little babies and the sandy windswept shores of Moonlight Beach! I hope that after reading Adam Chase's story, you'll get the feel of the ultimate in beach living. He has the coolest house on the beach, of course, being the reclusive architect who has designed a row of mansions along the shore. I can't even tell you how much fun it was for me to build this house from the ground up, in my imagination.

Living in southern California, I know something about beaches. I'm lucky enough to live just a canyon away from the Pacific shoreline, and on a good day, I'm there in thirty minutes. The beach has always refueled my engine when the tank goes empty. (You'd be surprised how often that happens!)

And if you know anything about me, you know I love babies. They're sweet and innocent and so lovable. Oh, really? Not our baby Rose. You see, she's got a problem with Adam, and she puts him to the daddy test, time and time again. Mia D'Angelo, the baby's guardian, does her share of "testing" gorgeous Adam Chase, too. Even when Adam comes dashing to her rescue and sparks ignite on the moonlit beach, Mia doesn't know if she can trust him with the most precious thing in her life: sweet baby Rose.

Welcome back to Moonlight Beach. I hope you're enjoying the series so far. Remember, *Her Forbidden Cowboy* (Zane Williams's story) was released in February 2015, and fabulous superstar Dylan McKay's story will be coming next.

Happy reading!

Charlene

THE BILLIONAIRE'S DADDY TEST

CHARLENE SANDS

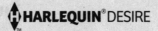

HARLEQUIN® DESIRE

Recycling programs
for this product may
not exist in your area.

ISBN-13: 978-0-373-73396-5

The Billionaire's Daddy Test

Copyright © 2015 by Charlene Swink

Printed in U.S.A.

Charlene Sands is a *USA TODAY* bestselling author of more than thirty-five romance novels, writing sensual contemporary romances and stories of the Old West. Her books have been honored with a National Readers' Choice Award, a CataRomance Reviewers' Choice Award, and she's a double recipient of the Booksellers' Best Award. She belongs to the Orange County chapter and the Los Angeles chapter of RWA.

Charlene writes "hunky heroes with heart." She knows a little something about true romance—she married her high school sweetheart! When not writing, Charlene enjoys sunny Pacific beaches, great coffee, reading books from her favorite authors and spending time with her family. You can find her on Facebook and Twitter. Charlene loves to hear from her readers! You can write her at PO Box 4883, West Hills, CA 91308, or sign up for her newsletter for fun blogs and ongoing contests at charlenesands.com.

Books by Charlene Sands

HARLEQUIN DESIRE

Moonlight Beach Bachelors

Her Forbidden Cowboy
The Billionaire's Daddy Test

The Slades of Sunset Ranch

Sunset Surrender
Sunset Seduction
The Secret Heir of Sunset Ranch
Redeeming the CEO Cowboy

The Worths of Red Ridge

Carrying the Rancher's Heir
The Cowboy's Pride
Worth the Risk

Visit the Author Profile page at Harlequin.com, or charlenesands.com, for more titles!

To the two new babies in my life!
You are welcomed and loved so much.
With four "princesses" now, you and your sisters
have made my "baby" research so much fun!
I am truly blessed.

One

Adam Chase had a right to know his baby daughter.

Mia couldn't deny that, but her heart still bled as if a dozen knives were piercing her. Darn her conscience for leading her to Moonlight Beach this morning. Her toes sifted through sand as she walked along the shoreline, flip-flops in hand. It was cooler than she'd expected; the fog flowing in from the sea coated the bright beach with a layer of gloom. Was it an omen? Had she made the wrong choice in coming here today? The image of Rose's innocent little face popped into her mind. Sweet Cheeks, she called her, because she had the rosiest cheeks of any baby Mia had ever seen. Her lips were perfectly pink, and when she'd smiled her first little baby smile, Mia had melted.

Rose was all Mia had left of her sister, Anna.

Mia shifted her gaze to the ocean. Just as she'd hoped, she spotted a male figure swimming way beyond the breaking waves hitting the shore. He was doing laps as if there were roped-off columns keeping him on point. If the scant research she'd found was anything to go by, it was surely him. Adam Chase, world-class architect, lived at the beach, was a recluse by nature and an avid swimmer. It only made sense he'd do his daily laps early, before the beach was populated.

A breeze lifted her hair, and goose bumps erupted on her arms. She shivered, partly from the cold, but also because what she came here to do was monumental. She'd have to be made of stone not to be frightened right now.

She didn't know what she'd say to him. She'd rehearsed a thousand and one lines, but never once had she practiced the truth.

With another glance at the water, she spotted him swimming in. Her throat tightened. It was time for the show, whatever that was. Mia was good at thinking on her feet. She calculated her steps carefully, so she'd intersect with him on the sand. Her hair lifted in the breeze, and another shiver racked her body. He stopped swimming and rose up from the shallow water, his shoulders broad as a Viking's. Her heart thumped a little faster. He came forward in long smooth strides. She scanned his iron chest, rippled with muscle—all that grace and power. The few pictures she'd found in her research hadn't done him justice. He was out-and-out beautiful in a godly way and so very tall.

He shook his head, and the sun-streaked tendrils of his hair rained droplets down along his shoulders.

"Ow!" Something pricked her foot from underneath. Pain slashed the soft pad and a sharp sting burned. She grabbed her foot and plunked down in the sand. Blood spurted out instantly. Gently, she brushed the sticky sand away and gasped when she saw the damage. Her foot was cut, slashed by a broken beer bottle she spied sticking out of the earth like a mini-skyscraper. If she hadn't been gawking…

"Are you hurt?" The deep voice reverberated in her ears, and she lifted her eyes to Adam Chase's concerned face.

"Oh, uh." She nodded. "Yes. I'm cut."

"Damn kids," he said, glancing at the broken bottle. He took her hand and placed it on the bridge of her foot. "Put pressure here and hang on a sec. I'll be right back."

"Th-thanks."

She applied pressure, squeezing her foot tight. It began to feel a little better, and the stinging dissipated. She glimpsed Adam as he jogged away. Her rescuer was just as appealing from the backside. Tanned legs, perfect butt and a strong back. She sighed. It was hardly the way she'd hoped to meet the very private Adam Chase, but it would have to do.

He returned a few seconds later holding a navy-blue-and-white beach towel. He knelt by her side. "Okay, I'm going to wrap it. That should stop the bleeding."

A huge wave crashed onto the shore, and water washed over her thighs. Adam noticed, his gaze darting through amazingly long lashes and roving over her legs. A warm rush of heat entered her belly. She wore white cotton shorts and a turquoise tank top. She'd wanted to appear like any other beachgoer taking a leisurely morning stroll along the water's edge, when in fact she'd deliberated over what to wear this morning for thirty minutes.

Now Adam Chase was touching her cautiously. His head down and a few strands of hair falling on his forehead, he performed the task as if it were an everyday occurrence. She had to admire him. "You seem to know what you're doing."

"Three years lifeguarding will do that to you." He glanced up and smiled, flashing a beautiful set of white teeth.

That smile buoyed her spirit a little.

"I'm Adam," he said.

"Mia."

"Nice to meet you, Mia."

"Uh, same here."

He finished his work, and her foot was tied tightly but with an excess of material hanging down. She'd never be able to walk away with any dignity. The makeshift tourniquet was ugly and cumbersome, but it seemed to do the trick. The bleeding was contained.

"Do you live close by?" he asked.

"Not really. I thought I'd go for a stroll along the beach this morning."

"Do you have any beach gear?"

She nodded. "It's about a mile up the beach." She pointed north. "That way."

Adam sat up on his knees and peered down at her, rubbing the back of his neck. "You really should have that cleaned and bandaged right away. It's a sizable gash."

She shivered. "Okay."

The water crept up to their legs again.

Adam frowned and glanced at her encumbered foot.

Pushing off from the sand, she tried to rise. "Oh!" Putting her weight on her foot burned like crazy. She bit her lip to keep from crying out any more and lowered herself back down onto the sand.

Adams's eyes softened. "Listen, I know we've just met, but I live right over there." He gestured to the biggest modern mansion on the beach. "I promise you, I'm not a serial killer or anything, but I have antiseptic and bandages in my house, and I can have you patched up pretty quickly."

Mia glanced around. No one else was on the beach. Wasn't this what she'd wanted? A chance to get to know Adam Chase? She knew darn well he wasn't a serial killer. All she knew was that he liked his privacy, he didn't go out much and—most important of all—he was Rose's father.

She could write volumes about what she didn't know about Adam Chase. And that's exactly why she'd come here—to find out what kind of man he truly was.

Rose's future was riding on it.

"I guess that would be okay."

Come to think of it, no one knew where she was today. Rose was with her great-grandmother. If Adam did have evil on his mind, it would be a long time before anyone came looking...

The mountain of a man scooped her up, and she gasped. *Pay attention, Mia.* Her pulse sped as he nestled her into his chest. His arms secure about her body, he began to carry her away from the water's edge. On instinct, she roped her arms around his neck. Water drops remained on his shoulders, cooling his skin where her hands entwined.

"Comfy?" A wry smile pulled at his lips.

Speechless, she nodded and gazed into his eyes. There were steely flecks layered over gray irises, soulful shadows and as mysterious as a deep water well. Oddly, she didn't feel *un*comfy in his arms, even though they were complete strangers.

"Good. Couldn't think of a faster way to get you to the house."

"Thank you?" she squeaked.

He didn't respond, keeping his eyes straight ahead. She relaxed a little until her foot throbbed. Little jabs of pain wound all around the bottom of her foot. She stifled a shriek when a few bright red drops of blood seeped from the towel onto the sand.

"Does it hurt?" he asked.

"Yes, this is…*awful*." She barely got the word out. Adam Chase or not, she wanted to crawl into a hole. What a way to meet a man. Any minute now, she'd probably bleed all over his gorgeous house.

"Awful?" He seemed to take exception with that. She wasn't complaining about his sudden caveman move, how he'd plucked her into his arms so easily. No, that part had been, well, amazing. But she felt like a helpless wounded animal. She couldn't even stand on her own two feet.

"Embarrassing," she muttered.

"No need to be embarrassed."

His stride was long and smooth as he moved over the sand toward his mansion. Up close, the detail of his craft showed in the trim of wide expansive windows, the texture of the stucco, the unique decorative double glass doors and the liberating feel of an outdoor living space facing the ocean—a billionaire's version of a veranda. Fireplaces, sitting areas with circular couches, overhead beams and stone floors all made up the outskirts of his house. The veranda was twice the size of her little Santa Monica apartment, and that was only a fraction of what she could see. Inside must be magnificent.

"Here we are," he said, steps away from the dream house.

"Uh, do you think we could stay out here?" She pointed to the enormous outside patio.

He blinked, those dark gray eyes twinkling. "Sure. If you feel safer outside."

"Oh no, it's not that."

His perfectly formed eyebrows arched upward. "No?"

"I don't want to ruin your carpeting or anything." Lord knew, she made a decent living at First Clips, but if she destroyed something in the mansion, it could take years to pay off a replacement.

"My carpet?" His smile could melt Mount Shasta. "There's not a shred of carpet in the house. I promise to keep you away from any rugs lying about."

"Oh, uh. Fine then."

He moved through the front doors easily and entered a massive foyer, where inlaid marble and intricate stone patterns led to a winding staircase. She gulped at the tasteful opulence. She clamped her mouth shut and held back a sigh from her lips. Was it the unexpected nuances she found in his stunning home, or was it the man himself who caused such a flurry in the pit of her stomach? His size commanded attention, the breadth of his shoulders, the bronze tone of his skin and, yes, the fact that he was shirtless and wet, his moisture clinging to her own clothes, his hands gripping the backs of her thighs.

A thrill ran through her, overriding her embarrassment.

He began to climb the stairs.

"Where are we going?" Up to his lair?

"The first aid supplies are in my bathroom. Mary is out shopping, or I'd have her go get them for us."

"Mary? Your girlfriend?"

His gaze slipped over to her. "My housekeeper."

"Oh." *Of course.*

"Have you lived here long?" She needed lessons in small talk.

"Long enough."

"The house is beautiful. Did you decorate it yourself?"

"I had some help."

Evasive but not rude. "I'm sorry about this. You probably have better things to do than play nursemaid to me."

"Like I said, I have mad lifeguarding skills."

Yes. Yes, he did.

Adam set the woman down on the bathroom counter. Long black lashes lifted and almond-shaped eyes, green as a spring meadow, followed his every movement. From what he could tell, she didn't have an ounce of makeup on her face. She didn't need it. Her beauty seemed natural, her face delicately sculpted, glowing in warm tones. Her mouth was shaped like a heart in the most subtle way, and her skin was soft as butter. His palms still tingled from holding the underside of her thighs as he'd lifted her off the hot sand. "Here we go. Just let me get a shirt and my glasses."

He grabbed the first shirt he found in his bedroom drawer and then came up with a pair of wire-rimmed glasses. Next he selected the medical supplies he'd need out of a closet in his bathroom. He found what he needed easily: gauze, peroxide, antibacterial cream. When it came to keeping things organized, he was meticulous. It was the way he rolled, and he'd taken more than a fair share of heat about it from everyone who knew him. That aside, he'd bet he'd shock his college pals if they saw the worn, tattered and faded to ghost-blue UCLA Bruin T-shirt he'd just thrown on. Adam almost cracked a smile. It was so unlike him; yet once a Bruin, always a Bruin. He wouldn't part with his shirt. He set his glasses onto the bridge of his nose. "Okay. Here goes. Ready?"

She nodded. "Go ahead."

Gently, he unwound the towel from her foot. "I want to take a better look at that gash."

"You're really nice for doing this," she said softly.

"Hmm."

"What kind of work do you do?" she asked.

He didn't take his eyes off her foot. It was small and delicate, and he was careful with her, surveying the damage and elevating the heel. "Uh, I'm self-employed."

"It's just that, well, this house is magnificent."

"Thank you."

"Is it just you and Mary living here?"

"Sometimes. Mia, do you think you could swivel the rest of your body up on the counter, near the sink, so I can see the foot a little better?"

"I think so." Holding the heel of her foot, he helped guide her legs onto the counter. She had to scoot back and pivot a bit until she filled half the length of the long cocoa marble commode. She couldn't be more than five foot five. Her foot hovered over the sink.

A tank top and white shorts showed off her sun-kissed body. Her legs were long and lean like a dancer's. Seeing her sprawled out before him, the entire Mia package was first-class gorgeous. He caught himself staring at her reflection. *Focus, Adam. Be a Good Samaritan.*

"So you went to UCLA?" she asked.

"Yeah. Undergrad." He stroked his chin and hesitated, staring at her foot. It had been years since his lifeguarding days. He'd never had qualms about giving first aid before. He'd done it a hundred times, including giving CPR to a man in his sixties. That hadn't been fun, but the man had survived and, years later, gratefully commissioned Adam to design a resort home on the French Riviera. It had been one of his first big architectural projects. But this was different somehow, with Mia, the beauty who had landed at his feet on the beach.

"Adam?"

He looked at her. A fleeting thought entered his head. For a woman in distress, she sure asked a lot of questions. It wouldn't be the first time someone tried an unorthodox way to interview him. But surely not Mia. Her foot was slashed pretty badly. Some women liked to talk when they were nervous. Did he make her nervous?

"Is it okay if I wash your foot?"

Her lovely olive complexion colored, and a flash of hesitation entered her eyes. "Do you have a foot fetish or anything?"

He grinned. Maybe he did make her nervous. "Nope. No fetishes at all."

She made a little noise when she inhaled. "Good to know. Okay."

He filled the sink with warm water. "Let me know if it hurts."

She nodded, squeezed her eyes shut and clenched her legs.

"Try to relax, Mia."

Her expression softened, and she opened her eyes. He rotated her slim ankle over the sink with one hand and splashed warm water onto her foot. Using a dollop of antibacterial liquid soap, he cleansed the area thoroughly with a soft washcloth. Heat rose up his neck. It was about as intimate as he'd been with a woman in months, and Mia, with her cotton-candy-pink toenails, endless legs and beautiful face was 100 percent woman. "The good news is, the bleeding has stopped."

"Wonderful. Now I can stop worrying about destroying your furniture."

"Is that what you're worried about?" He furrowed his brow.

"After the foot fetish thing, yes."

He shook his head and fought the smile trying to break his concentration. Not too many people made him smile, and Mia had already done that several times. "You can stop worrying. I don't think you'll need stitches either. Luckily, the gash isn't as deep as it looked. It's long, though, and it might be painful for you to walk on for a day or two. You can have a doctor take a look, just to make sure."

She said nothing.

He dabbed the cut with peroxide, and bubbles clustered up. Next he lathered her wound with antibiotic cream.

"How're you doing?" He lifted his head, and her face was there, so close, obviously watching his ministrations. Their eyes met, and he swallowed hard. He could swim a mile in her pretty green eyes.

She took a second to answer. "I'm, uh, doing well."

It was quiet in the house, just the two of them, Adam's hand clamping her ankle gently. "That's…good. I'll be done in a second." He cleared his throat and picked up the bandages. "I'm going to wrap this kind of tight."

He caught Mia glancing at his left hand, focusing on his ring finger, as in no white tan lines, and then her lips curled up. "I'm ready."

Suddenly, he'd never been happier that he was romantically unattached than right at that moment.

After Adam had patched her up, Mia's stomach had shamefully grumbled as he'd helped her down from the bathroom counter. She'd probably turned ten shades of red when the unladylike sound echoed against the walls. Luckily, he'd only smiled and had graciously invited her to breakfast. She had to keep her foot elevated for a little while, he'd said, and Mia had been more than willing to continue to spend time with him.

To get the scoop on him. It would take some doing; he was tight-lipped. Making conversation was not in his wheelhouse. But so many other things were. Like the way he'd immediately come to her aid on the beach, how thoughtful he'd been afterward, carrying her into his house, and how deadly handsome he looked behind those wire-rimmed glasses. *Oh, Mama!*

She sat in a comfortable chaise chair in the open-air terrace off a kitchen a chef would dream about. Part of the terrace was shaded by an overhead balcony. Adam was seated to her right at the table. Her foot was propped on another chair. Both faced the Pacific.

The morning gloom was beginning to lift, the sun breaking through and the sound of waves hitting the shore penetrating her ears. White curtains billowed behind her as she sipped coffee from a gold-rimmed china cup. Adam knew how to live. It was all so decadent, except that Adam, for all his good looks and obvious wealth, seemed down-to-earth even if he didn't talk about himself much. And she had to admit, her Viking warrior looked more like a beach bum in khaki shorts and a beaten-down Bruins T-shirt. But she still hadn't found out much about him.

"So you work as a hairdresser?" he said.

"Actually, I own the shop but I don't cut hair. I have two employees who do." She gauged his reaction and didn't elaborate that First Clips, her shop, catered to children. The hairdressers wore costumes and the little girls sat on princess thrones, while the boys sat in rocket ships to have their hair cut. Afterward, the newly groomed kids were rewarded with tiaras or rocket goggles. Mia was proud of their business. Anna had developed the idea and had been the main hairstylist while Mia ran the financial end of things. She had to be careful about what she revealed about First Clips. If Anna had confided in him about their business, he might connect the dots and realize Mia wasn't exactly an innocent bystander out for a beach stroll this morning.

Mary, his sixtysomething housekeeper, approached the table and served platters of poached eggs, maple bacon, fresh biscuits and an assortment of pastries.

"Thank you," she said. "The coffee is delicious." Adam had brought it out from the kitchen earlier.

"Mary, this is Mia," he said. "She had an accident on the beach this morning."

"Oh, dear." Mary's kind pale blue eyes darted to her bandaged foot. "Are you all right?"

"I think I will be, thanks to Adam. I stepped on a broken bottle."

Mary shook her head. "Those stupid kids…always hanging around after dark." Her hand went to her mouth immediately. "Sorry. It's just that they're in high school and shouldn't be drinking beer and doing who knows what else on the beach. Adam has talked about having them arrested."

"Maybe I should," he muttered, and she got the idea he wasn't fully committed to the idea. "Or maybe I'll teach them a lesson."

"How?" Mary asked.

"I've got a few things bouncing around in my head."

"Well, I wish you would," she said, and Mia got the impression Mary had some clout in Adam's household. "It's very nice to meet you, Mia."

"Nice meeting you, too."

"Thanks, Mary. The food looks delicious," he said. Mary retreated to the kitchen, and Adam pointed to the dishes of food. "Dig in. I know you're hungry." His lips twitched. When he smiled, something pinged inside her.

She fixed herself a plate of eggs and buttered a biscuit, leaving the bacon and pastries aside, while Adam filled his plate with a little of everything. "So you said you're self-employed. What kind of work do you do?"

He slathered butter onto his biscuit. "I design things," he said, then filled his mouth and chewed.

"What kind of things?" she pressed. The man really didn't like talking about himself.

He shrugged. "Homes, resorts, villas."

She bit into her eggs and leaned back, contemplating. "I bet you do a lot of traveling."

"Not really."

"So you're a homebody?"

He shrugged again. "It's not a bad thing, is it?"

"No, I'm sort of a homebody myself, actually." Now that she was raising Rose, she didn't have time for anything other than work and baby. It was fine by her. Her heart ached every time she thought about giving Rose up. She didn't know if she could do it. Meeting Adam was the first step, and she almost didn't want to take any more. Why couldn't he have been a loser? Why couldn't he have been a jerk? And why on earth was she so hopelessly attracted to him?

Had he been married? Did he have a harem of girlfriends? Or any nasty habits, like drugs or gambling or a sex addiction? Mia's mind whirled with possibilities, but nothing seemed to suit him. But wasn't that what people said about their neighbors when it was discovered they were violent terrorists or killers? "He seemed like such a nice man, quiet, kept to himself."

Okay, so her imagination was running wild. She still didn't know enough about Adam. She'd have to find a way to spend more time with him.

Rose was worth the trouble.

Rose was worth…everything.

"You're not going to be able to walk back," Adam said.

She glanced at her foot still elevated on the chair. Breakfast was over, and her heart started thumping against her chest the way it did just before panic set in. She needed more time. She hadn't found out anything personal about Adam yet, other than he was filthy rich and truly had mad first aid skills. Her foot was feeling much better, wrapped tightly, but she hadn't tried to get up yet. Adam had carried her to her seat on the shaded veranda.

She knew her flip-flops would flop. She couldn't walk in them in the sand, not with the bandage on her foot.

"I don't have a choice."

Adam cocked his head to the side, and his lips twisted. "I have a car, you know."

She began shaking her head. "I can't impose on your day any more. I'll get back on my own."

She pulled her legs down and scooted her chair back as she rose. "You've already done en—" Searing jabs pricked at the ball of her foot. She clenched her teeth and keeled to the right, taking pressure off the wound. She grabbed for the table, and Adam was beside her instantly, his big hands bracing her shoulders.

"Whoa. See, I didn't think you could walk."

"I, uh." Her shoulders fell. "Maybe you're right."

And for the third time today, she was lifted up in Adam's strong arms. He'd excused himself while Mary was cooking breakfast and taken a quick shower and now his scent wafted to her nose—a strong, clean, entirely too sexy smell that floated all around her.

"This is getting to be a habit," she said softly.

He made a quick adjustment, tucking her gently in again, and gave her a glance. "It's necessary."

"And you always do what's necessary?"

"I try to."

He began walking, then stopped and bent his body so she could grab her turquoise flip-flops off the kitchen counter. "Got them?"

"I got them."

"Hang on."

She was. Clinging to him and enjoying the ride.

Two

Adam carried Mia down a long corridor heading to the garage. After traveling about twenty steps, the hallway opened to a giant circular room and a streamlined convertible Rolls-Royce popped into her line of vision. The car, a work of art in itself, was parked showroom-style in the center of the round room. She'd never seen such luxury before and was suddenly stunningly aware of the vast differences between Adam Chase and Mia D'Angelo.

She took her eyes off the car and scanned the room. A gallery of framed artwork hung on the surrounding walls and her gaze stopped on a brilliant mosaic mural that encompassed about one-third of the gallery. Her mouth hung open in awe. She pressed her lips together tightly and hoped her gawking wasn't noticed.

"Adam, you have your own bat cave?"

His lips twitched. He surveyed the room thoughtfully. "No one's ever described it quite like that before," he said.

"How many people have seen this?"

"Not many."

"Ah, so it *is* your bat cave. You keep it a secret."

"I had this idea when I was designing the house and it wouldn't leave me alone. I had to see it through."

Score one for his perseverance.

"I don't know much about great works of art, but this gallery is amazing. Are you an art junkie?" she asked.

"More like I appreciate beauty. In all forms." His eyes

touched over her face, admiring, measuring and thoughtful. Heat prickled at the back of her neck. If he was paying her a compliment, she wouldn't acknowledge it verbally. She couldn't help it if having a gorgeous man hold her in her arms and whisper sweet words in her ear made her bead up with sweat. But she wasn't here to flirt, fawn or fantasize. She needed to finesse answers out of him. Period.

He stepped onto the platform that housed the car and opened the passenger door of the Rolls-Royce. "What are you doing?"

"Taking you home."

"In this? How? I mean, the car's a part of your gallery. And in case you haven't noticed, there's no garage door anywhere." She double-checked her surroundings. No, she wasn't mistaken. But just in case the bat cave had secret walls, she asked, "Is there?"

"No, no garage door, but an elevator."

Again her gaze circled the room. "Where?"

"We're standing on it. Now let me get you into the car."

Buttery leather seats cushioned her bottom as he lowered her into the Rolls, his beautiful Nordic face inches from her. The scent of him surrounded her in a halo of arousing aroma. Her breath hitched, she hoped silently. Mia, stop drooling.

"Can you manage the seat belt?" he asked.

Her foot was all bandaged up, not her hands, but still a fleeting thought touched her mind of Adam gently tucking her into the seat belt. "Of course."

He backed away and came around to the other end of the car and climbed in. "Ready?"

"For?"

"Don't be alarmed. We're going to start moving down."

He pressed a few buttons, and noises that sounded like a plane's landing gear opening up, filled the room. Mia had a faint notion that they were going to take off somehow. But then the platform began a slow and easy descent as the main floor of Adam's house began to disappear. Grandma Tess would call it an "E" ticket ride.

She looked up and the ceiling was closing again, kind of like the Superdome. Adam's gallery had a replacement floor. If he designed this, he was certainly an architectural and mechanical genius.

Score one more for Adam Chase.

Smooth as glass, they landed in a garage on the street level. More noises erupted, she imagined to secure the car elevator onto the ground floor. Inside the spacious garage, three other cars were parked. "Were these cars out of gas?" she asked.

A chuckle rumbled from his throat. "I thought this would be fastest and easier for you. And to be honest, it's been a while since I've taken the Rolls out."

She liked honesty, but surely he wasn't trying to impress her? He'd already done that the second he'd strode out of the ocean and come to her aid.

A Jag, an all-terrain Jeep and a little sports car were outdone by the Rolls, yet she wouldn't turn any one of them down if offered. "So, are you a car fanatic?"

He revved the engine and pressed the remote control. The garage door opened, and sunshine poured in. "So many questions, Mia. Just sit back, stretch out your leg and enjoy the ride."

What choice did she have? Adam clearly didn't like talking about himself. Anna's dying words rang in her head and seized her heart. Clutching her sister's hand, her plea had been weak but so determined. "Adam Chase, the baby's real father. Architect. One night…that's all I know. Find him."

Anna had been more adventurous than Mia, but now she understood why she'd known little about the man who'd fathered her child. Anna had probably done most of the talking. It had been during the lowest part of her sister's life, when she thought she'd lost Edward forever. Maybe neither one of them had done much talking.

She glanced at Adam's profile as he put the car in gear, his wrist resting on the steering wheel. Chiseled cheekbones, thoughtful gray eyes, strong jaw. His hair, kissed by the sun, was cropped short and straight. No rings on his fingers. Again, she wondered if he had a girlfriend or three. Everything about him, his house, his cars, his good looks, screamed babe magnet, yet oddly, her gut was telling her something different, something she couldn't put her finger on. And that's why she had to find a way to delay her departure. She didn't have enough to go on. She certainly couldn't turn her sweet-cheeked baby Rose over to him. Not yet.

He might not even want her.

Perish the thought. Who wouldn't want that beautiful baby?

"Are you sure you don't want me to drive you home?" he asked. "You can have someone pick up your car later if you can't drive comfortably."

"Oh no. Please. Just drive me to my car. It's not that far, and I'm sure I can drive."

Adam took his eyes off the road and turned to her. "Okay, if you're sure." He didn't seem convinced.

"My foot's feeling better already. I'm sure."

He nodded and sighed, turning his attention back to the road.

"How far?"

"I'm parked at lifeguard station number three."

"Got it."

It was less than a mile, and she kept her focus on the glossy waters of Moonlight Beach as he drove the rest of the way in silence. Too soon, they entered the parking lot. "There's my car." She pointed to her white Toyota Camry. He pulled up next to it. The Rolls looked out of place in a parking lot full of soccer-mom vans and family sedans. A mustard-yellow school bus was unloading a gaggle of giggling children.

"Hang on," he said. "I'll get your gear. Just show me where it is on the beach."

Whoops. She'd lied about that. She didn't have so much as a beach towel on the sand. Blinking, she stalled for time. "Oh, I guess I forgot. I must have put everything in my trunk before I took my walk."

Adam didn't seem fazed, and she sighed, relieved. He climbed out of the car, jaunted around the front end of the Rolls and stopped on the passenger side. She opened the car door, and he was there, ready to help her out.

His hands were on her again, lifting her, and a warm jolt catapulted down to her belly. She'd never felt anything quite like it before, this fuzzy don't-stop-touching-me kind of sensation that rattled her brain and melted her insides.

He set her down, and she put weight on her foot. "I'm okay," she said, gazing into eyes softened by concern.

"You're sure?"

"If you can just help me to my car, I'll be fine."

He wrapped his arm around her waist, and there it was again—warm, gooey sensations swimming through her body. She half hopped, half walked as he carefully guided her to the driver's side of the car.

"Your keys?" he asked.

She dug her hand into the front pocket of her shorts and came up with her car key. "Right here."

He stared at her. "Well, then. You're set."

"Yes."

Neither one of them moved. Not a muscle. Not a twitch. Around them noises of an awakening beach pitched into the air, children's laughter, babies crying, the roar of the waves hitting the shore, seagulls squawking, and still, it was as if they were alone. The beating of her heart pounded in her skull. Adam wasn't going to say anything more, although some part of her believed he wanted to.

She rose up on tiptoes, lifted her eyes fully to his and

planted a kiss on his cheek. "Thank you, Adam. You've been very sweet."

His mouth wrenched up. "Welcome."

"I'd love to repay you for your kindness by cooking you one of my grandmother's favorite Tuscan dishes, but—"

"But?" His brows arched. He seemed interested, thank goodness.

"My stove is on the blink." Not exactly a lie. Two burners were out and the oven *was* temperamental.

He shook his head. "There's no need to repay me for anything."

Her hopes plummeted, yet she kept a smile on her face.

"But I love Italian food, so how about cooking that meal at my place when you're up to it?"

At his place? In that gorgeous state-of-the-art kitchen? Thank goodness for small miracles. "I'd love to. Saturday night around seven?" That would give her three days to heal.

"Sounds good."

It was a date. Well, not a date.

She was on a mission and she couldn't forget that.

Even if her mouth still tingled from the taste of his skin on her lips.

Adam removed his glasses and set them down on the drafting table. He leaned back in his seat and sighed. His tired eyes needed a rest. He closed them and pinched the bridge of his nose as seconds ticked by. How long had he been at it? He turned his wrist and glanced at his watch. Seven hours straight. The villa off the southern coast of Spain he was designing was coming along nicely. But his eyes were crossing, and not even the breezes blowing into his office window were enough to keep him focused. He needed a break.

And it was all because of a beautiful woman named Mia. He'd thought of her often these past two days. It wasn't often a woman captured his imagination anymore. But somehow this beautiful woman intrigued him. Spending those few hours with her had made him realize how isolated he'd become lately.

He craved privacy. But he hadn't minded her interrupting his morning, or her nosy questions. Actually, coming to her aid was the highlight of his entire week. He was looking forward to their evening together tomorrow night.

"Adam, you have a phone call," Mary said, bringing him his cell phone. Few people had his private number, and he deliberately let Mary answer most of the calls when he was working. "It's your mother."

He always took his mother's calls. "Thanks," he said, and Mary handed him the phone. "Hi, Mom."

"Adam, how's my firstborn doing today?"

Adam's teeth clenched. The way she referred to him was a constant reminder that there had once been three of them and that Lily was gone.

"I'm doing okay. Just finished the day's work."

"The villa?"

"Yeah. I'm happy with the progress."

"Sometimes I can't get over that you design the most fascinating places."

"I have a whole team, Mom. It's not just me."

"It's your company, Adam. You've done remarkable things with your life."

He pinched the bridge of his nose again. His mother never came right out and told him she was proud of him. Maybe she was, but he'd never heard the words and he probably never would. He couldn't blame her. He'd failed in doing the one thing that would've made her proud of him, the one thing that would've cemented her happy life. Instead, he'd caused his family immense grief.

"Have you spoken with your brother yet?"

He knew this was coming. He braced himself.

"Not yet, but I plan to speak with Brandon this week."

"It's just that I'm hoping you two reconcile your differences. My age is creeping up on me, you know. And it's something I've been praying for, Adam…for you and Brandon to act like brothers again."

"I know, Mom." The only justice was that he knew his mother was giving Brandon the very same plea. She wanted what was left of her family to be whole again. "I've put in a few calls to him. I'm just waiting to hear back."

"I understand he's in San Francisco, but he'll be home tonight." Home was Newport Beach for his brother. He was a pilot and now ran a charter airline company based out of Orange County. He and Brandon never saw eye to eye on anything. They were as different as night and day. Maybe that's why Jacqueline, his ex-girlfriend, had gotten involved with his brother. She craved excitement. She loved adventure. Adam would never be convinced that she hadn't left him for Brandon. Brandon was easygoing and free-spirited, while Adam remained guarded, even though he'd loved Jacqueline with all of his heart.

"Don't worry, Mom, I'll work it out with Brandon. He wouldn't want to miss your birthday party. We both know how important it is to you."

"I want my boys to be close again."

Adam couldn't see that happening. But he'd make sure Brandon would come to celebrate their mother's seventieth birthday and the two of them would be civil to one another. "I understand."

It was the best he could do. He couldn't make promises to his mother about his relationship with Brandon. There was too much pain and injury involved.

"Well, I'd better say goodbye. I've got a big day tomorrow. A field trip to the Getty Museum. It's been a few years since I've been there."

"Okay, Mom. Is Ginny going?"

"Of course. She's my Sunny Hills partner. We do everything together."

"And you haven't gotten on each other's nerves yet?"

A warmhearted chuckle reached his ears. It was a good sound. One he didn't hear enough from his mother. "Oh, we have our moments. Ginny can be overbearing at times. But she's my best friend and next-door neighbor, and we do so love the same things."

"Okay, Mom. Well, have fun tomorrow."

"Thanks, dear."

"I'll be in touch."

Adam hung up the phone, picturing his mom at Sunny Hills Resort. It was a community for active seniors, inland and just ten miles away from Moonlight Beach. Thankfully his mother hadn't balked about leaving Oklahoma and the life she'd always known after his father died. Adam had bought her a home in the gated community, and she seemed to have settled in quite nicely, her middle America manners and charm garnering her many friendships. The activities there kept her busy. He tried to see her at least once or twice a month.

Mary walked into his office. "It's dinnertime. Are you hungry, Adam?"

"I could eat. Sure."

"Would you like me to set you up on the veranda? Or inside the kitchen?"

"Kitchen's fine."

Mary nodded.

Mary asked him every night, and he always had the same answer for her, but he never wanted her to stop asking. Maybe one night he'd change his mind. Maybe one night he'd want to sit outside and see the sun set, hear distant laughter coming from the shoreline and let faint music reach his ears. Maybe one night he wouldn't want to eat in solitude, then watch a ball game and read himself to sleep.

"Oh, and Mary?"

She was almost out of the doorway when she turned. "Yes?"

"Take the day off tomorrow. Enjoy a long weekend."

Sundays and Mondays were her days off. Adam could fare for two days without housekeeping help, unless something important came up. He made sure it didn't. He had an office in the city where he met with his clients and had meetings with his staff. He often worked on his designs from home. His office was fully equipped with everything he needed.

"Thank you, Adam. Does this have anything to do with that lovely girl you met the other day?"

Mary had been with him since before he'd moved into his house. Some said she had no filter, but Adam liked her. She spoke her mind, and he trusted her, maybe more than some trusted their own relatives. She was younger than his mother but old enough to know the score. "If I told you yes, would you leave it at that?"

A hopeful gleam shined in her blue eyes. "A date?"

Of course she wouldn't leave it alone. "Not really. She's coming over to cook for me. As a thank-you for helping her."

Mary grinned, her face lighting up. "A date. I'll make sure the kitchen is well stocked."

"It's always well stocked, thanks to you, Mary. Don't worry about it. I imagine she's bringing over what she needs. So enjoy your Saturday off."

"And you enjoy your date," she said. "I'll go now and set the table for dinner."

She walked out of the room and Adam smiled. Mia was coming over to make him a meal. For all he knew, she felt obligated to reciprocate a favor. Not that what he'd done had been a favor; anyone with half a heart—that would be him—would've helped her out. Who wouldn't stop for a woman bleeding and injured on the beach?

A beautiful woman, with a knockout body and skin tones that made you want to touch and keep on touching.

He had to admit, the thought of her coming over tomorrow got his juices flowing.

And that hadn't happened in a very long time.

"Gram, this is so hard," Mia said, shifting her body to and fro, rocking baby Rose. The baby's weight drained her strength and stung her arms, but she didn't want to stop rocking her. She didn't want to give up one second of her time with Rose. Her sweet face was docile now, so very peaceful. She was a joy, a living, breathing replica of her mama. How could she lose Anna a second time? "I can't imagine not seeing her every day. I can't imagine giving her up."

"She's ours, too, you know." Grandma Tess sat in her favorite cornflower-blue sofa chair. As she smiled her encouragement the wrinkles around her eyes deepened. "We won't really be giving her up," she said softly. "I'm sure… this Adam, he'll do the right thing. He'll allow you contact with the baby."

"Allow." A frown dragged at her lips. She'd raised Rose from birth. They'd bonded. Now someone would have the power to *allow* her to see Rose?

"He may not be the father, after all. Have you thought about that?"

"I have," she said, her hips swinging gently. "But my gut's telling me he's the one. Rose has his eyes. And his hair coloring. She's not dark like us."

"Well, then, maybe you should get going. Lay the baby down in the playpen. She'll probably sleep most of the night. We'll be fine—don't you worry."

"I know. She loves you, Gram." Tears formed in her eyes. Her heart was so heavy right now. She didn't want to leave. She didn't want to see Adam Chase tonight. She wanted to stay right here with Rose and Gram. She caught the moisture dripping from her eyes with a finger and sighed. "I won't be late. And if you need me for anything, call my cell. I'll keep it handy."

She laid the baby down in the playpen that served as the crib in Gram's house. Wearing a bubblegum-pink sleep sack, Rose looked so cozy, so content. Mia curled a finger around the baby's hair and, careful not to wake her, whispered, "Good night, Sweet Cheeks."

She left the baby's side to lean down to kiss Gram's cheek. Her skin was always warm and supple and soft like a feather down pillow. "Don't bother getting up. I'll lock you in."

"Okay, sweetheart. Don't forget the groceries."

"I won't," she said.

As she passed the hallway mirror, she gave herself a glance. She wore a coral sundress with an angled shoulder and a modest hemline. Her injured foot had healed enough for her to wear strappy teal-blue flat sandals that matched her teardrop necklace and earrings. Her hair was down and slight waves touched the center of her back.

"You look beautiful, Mia."

"Thanks, Gram." She lifted the bag of foodstuffs she'd need to make the meal, glanced at Rose one more time and then exited her grandmother's house, making sure to lock the door.

The drive to Adam Chase's estate was far too short. She reached his home in less than twenty minutes. Her nerves prickled as she entered the long driveway and pressed the gate button. After a few seconds, Adam's strong voice came over the speaker. "Mia?"

"Yes, hello... I'm here."

Nothing further was said as the wrought-iron gates slid away, concealing themselves behind a row of tall ivy scrubs. She drove on, her hands tight on the steering wheel, her heart pumping. She had half a mind to turn the car around and forget she'd ever met Adam Chase. If only she had the gumption to do that. He would never know he had produced a child. But how fair would that be to him or to Rose? Would she wonder why she didn't know her father and try to find him once she grew up? Would she pepper her aunt Mia with questions and live her life wondering about her true parents?

In her heart, Mia knew she was doing the right thing. But why did it have to hurt so much?

She parked her car near the front of the house on the circular drive. Adam waited for her on the steps of the elaborate front door, his hands in the pockets of dark slacks. Her breath hitched. A charcoal silk shirt hugged arms rippling with muscle and his silver-gray eyes met hers through the car window. Before she knew it, he was approaching and opening the car door for her. His scent wafted up, clean and subtly citrus.

"Hello, Mia." His deep voice penetrated her ears.

She took a breath to calm her nerves. "Hi."

"How are you?" he asked.

"I'm all healed up thanks to you."

"Good to hear. I've been looking forward to the meal you promised." He stretched his hand out to her and she took it. Enveloped in his warmth, she stepped out of the car.

"I hope I didn't overstate my talents."

His gaze flowed over her dress first and then sought the depth of her eyes. "I don't think you did." A second floated by. "You look very nice."

"Thank you."

He spied the grocery bag on the passenger seat and without pause lifted it out. "Ready?"

She gulped. "Yes."

He walked alongside her, slowing his gait to match hers. As they climbed wide marble steps, he reached for the door and pushed it open for her. Manners he had. Another plus for Adam Chase. "After you," he said, and once again she stepped inside his mansion.

"I still can't get over this home, Adam. The bat cave is

one thing, but the rest of this house is equally mind-blowing. I bet it was a dream of yours from early on, just like your gallery garage."

"Maybe it was."

He was definitely the king of ambiguity. Adam, guarded and private, never gave much away about himself. Already he was fighting her inquiries.

"I've got wine ready on the veranda, if you'd like a drink before you start cooking."

"We."

"Pardon me?"

"You're going to help me, Adam." Maybe she could get him to open up while chopping vegetables and mincing meat.

He rubbed the back of his neck. "I thought I'd just watch."

"That's no fun." She smiled. "You'll enjoy the meal more knowing you've participated."

"Okay," he said, nodding his head. "I'll try. But I'm warning you, I've never been too good in the kitchen."

"If you can design a house like this, you can sauté veggies. I'm sure of it."

He chuckled and his entire face brightened. Good to see. She followed him into the kitchen, where he set her bag down on an island counter nearly bigger than the entire kitchen in her apartment. Oh, it would be a thrill cooking in here.

"So what's the dish called?"

"Tagliatelle Bolognese."

"Impressive."

"It's delicious. Unless you're a vegetarian. Then you might have issues."

"You know I'm not."

She did know that much. They'd shared a meal together. "Well, since the sauce needs simmering for an hour or two, maybe we'll have our wine after we get the sauce going."

"Sounds like a plan. What should I do?"

She scanned his pristine clothing. "For one, take your shirt off."

A smile twitched at his lips. "Okay."

He reached for the top button on his shirt. After unfastening it, he unbuttoned the next and the next. Mia's throat went dry as his shirt gaped open, exposing a finely bronzed column of skin. She hadn't forgotten what he looked like without a shirt. Just three days ago he'd strode out of the sea, soaking wet, taking confident strides to come to her aid.

"Why am I doing this?" he asked finally. He was down to the fourth button.

Her gaze dipped again and she stared at his chest. "Because, uh, the sauce splatters sometimes. I wouldn't want you to ruin your nice shirt."

"And why aren't you doing the same? Taking off that beautiful dress?"

Her breath hitched. He was flirting, in a dangerous way. "Because," she said, digging into her bag and grabbing her protection. "I brought an apron."

She snapped her wrist and the apron unfolded. It was an over-the-head, tie-at-the-waist apron with tiny flowers that didn't clash with her coral dress. She put it on and tied the straps behind her back. "There. Why don't you change into a T-shirt or something?"

He nodded. "I'll be right back."

By the time Adam returned, she had all the ingredients in place. He wore a dark T-shirt now, with white lettering that spelled out Catalina Island. "Better?"

The muscles in his arms nearly popped out of the shirt. "Uh-huh."

"What now?" he asked.

"Would you mind cutting up the onions, celery and garlic?"

"Sure."

He grabbed a knife from a drawer and began with the

onions. While he was chopping away, she slivered pieces of pork and pancetta. "I'll need a frying pan," she said. Her gaze flew to the dozens of drawers and cabinets lining the walls. She'd gotten lucky; the chopping blocks and knives were on the countertop.

"Here, let me." Adam reached for a wide cabinet in front of her and grazed the tops of her thighs with his forearm as he opened the lower door. She froze for a second as a hot flurry swept through her lower parts. It was an accidental touch, but oh how her body had reacted. His fingertips simply touched the drawer loaded with shiny pots and pans and it slid open automatically. "There you go."

She stood, astonished. "I've never seen anything like that. You have a bat cave kitchen, too."

"It's automated, that's all. No pulling or yanking required."

"I think I'm in heaven." How wistful she sounded, her voice breathy.

Adam stood close, gazing at her in that way he had, as if trying to figure her out. His eyes were pure silver gray and a smidgen of blue surrounded the rims. They reminded her of a calm sea after a storm. "I think I am, too."

She blinked. His words fell from his lips sincerely, not so much heady flirtation but as if he'd been surprised, pleasantly. Her focus was sidetracked by compelling eyes, ego-lifting words and a hard swimmer's body. *Stop it, Mia. Concentrate. Think about Rose. And why you are here.*

She turned from him and both resumed their work. After a minute, she tossed the veggies into the fry pan, adding olive oil to the mix. The pan sizzled. "So, did you help your mother cook when you were a boy?" she asked.

Grandma Tess always said you could judge a man by the way he treated his mother.

"Nah, my mom would toss us boys out of the kitchen. Only Lily was— Never mind."

She turned away from the clarifying onions and steaming veggies to glance at his profile. A tic worked at his jaw, his face pinched. "Lily?"

"My sister. She's gone now. But to answer your question, no, I didn't help with meals much."

He'd had a sister, and now she was gone? Oh, she could relate to that. Her poor sweet Anna was also gone. He didn't want to talk about his sister. No great surprise. She'd already learned that Adam didn't like to talk about himself. "Do you have brothers?"

"One."

He didn't say more. It was like the proverbial pulling teeth to get answers from him.

She added the pork to the mix and stirred. "Did you grow up around here?" she asked matter-of-factly.

"No, did you?"

"I grew up not far from here. In the OC." She didn't like thinking about those times and how her family had been run out of town, thanks to her father. She, her mama and sister had had to leave their friends, their home and the only life they'd ever known because of James Burkel. Mia had cried for days. It wasn't fair, she kept screaming at her mother. But it hadn't been her mother's fault. Her mother had been a victim, too, and the scandal of her father's creation had besmirched the family name. The worst of it was that an innocent young girl had lost her life. "Here, stir this for me," she said to Adam, "if you wouldn't mind. We're caramelizing the meat and veggies now and don't want them to burn. I'll get the sauce."

"Sure." He grabbed the wooden spoon from her hands and stood like stone, his face tightly wound as he concentrated on stirring. She was sorry she'd made him uncomfortable with her questions. But they had to be asked.

"Okay, in goes the sauce. Stand back a little."

He turned her way. "What's that?"

She gripped a tube of tomato paste in her hand and squeezed. Red paste swirled out. "Tuscan toothpaste."

He laughed, surprised. "What?"

"That's what we call it. It's concentrated sauce. Very flavorful. Take a taste."

She sunk her spoon into the sauce and then brought it to his mouth. His lips parted, his head bent and his eyes stayed on hers as she gave him a taste. "Might be a little hot."

He swallowed, nodding his head. "It's so good."

"I know. Yummy."

His eyes twinkled. There was a moment of mischief, of teasing, and his smile quickened her heart. "Yummy," he repeated.

The staunch set of his jaw relaxed and she stared at his carefree expression. She liked the unguarded Adam best.

After tossing in the herbs and the rest of the ingredients, she set the pan to simmer and they left the kitchen for the open-air veranda. "I don't usually come out here," Adam said, pulling out a chair for her. "But I thought you might like it."

The sun was dipping, casting a shimmering glow on the water. Hues of grape and sherbet tangled through the sky. It was glorious. There was nothing better than a beachside view of the horizon at this time of day. "Why not, Adam? If I lived here, I'd spend every night watching the sunset."

"It's…" His face pinched tight again, and she couldn't figure out if it was pain or regret that kept him from saying more. Maybe it was both? "Never mind."

Lonely. Was that what he was going to say? Was this intelligent, wealthy, physically perfect specimen of man actually lonely?

"Would you like a glass of wine?"

"Yes," she answered.

"Cabernet goes well with Italian."

"It does."

He poured her a glass, and she waited for him before taking her first sip.

"Mmm. This is delicious."

The veranda spread out over the sand in a decking made entirely of white stone. A circular area designated the fire pit and off to the side, a large in-ground spa swirled with invigorating waters. She'd been here before, sat close to this very spot, but she'd been too immersed in her mission to really take note of the glorious surroundings. Sheer draperies billowed behind them.

"I'm glad you like it."

What was not to like? If only she could forget who Adam Chase really was.

They sipped wine and enjoyed the calm of the evening settling in. A few scattered beachgoers would appear, walking the sands in the distance, but other than that, they were completely alone.

"Why did you leave Orange County? For college?" he asked.

"No, it was before that." The wine was fruity and smooth and loosened her tongue, but she couldn't tell Adam the reason her mother had picked up and left their family home. She'd been careful not to share the closest things about herself to Adam, in case Anna had divulged some of their history to him. While Anna had kept the last name Burkel, Mia had legally changed her name to her mother's maiden name, D'Angelo, as an adult. Mia was dark haired with green eyes, while her sister had been lighter in complexion and bottle blonde. She wondered if Adam would even remember much about Anna. It had been a one-night fling, and a big mistake, according to Anna. "After my mother and father got divorced, we came to live with my grandmother."

It was close to the truth.

"I see. Where did you go to school?"

"I graduated from Santa Monica High and put myself through community college. I bet you have multiple degrees."

"A few," he admitted and then sipped his drink. His gaze turned to the sea.

"You're very talented. I'm curious. Why did you decide to become an architect?"

He shrugged, deep in thought. Oh no, not another evasive answer coming on. Was he trying to figure out a way out of her question? "I guess I wanted to build something tangible, something that wouldn't blow over in the wind."

"Like the three little pigs. You're the smart pig, building the house made of bricks."

His lips twitched again and he lifted his glass to his mouth. "You do have a way of putting things. I've never been compared to a pig before." He sipped his drink.

"A *smart* pig, don't forget that. You build structures that are sturdy as well as beautiful."

He nodded. "Foundation comes first. Then I layer in the beauty."

She smiled. "I like that."

He reached for her hand. "And I like you, Mia." The hand covering hers was strong and gentle.

His eyes were warm, darkening to slate gray and as liquid as the sensations sprinting through her body right now. This wasn't supposed to happen. This intense, hard-to-ignore feeling she got in the pit of her belly. She couldn't be attracted to him. It was impossible and would ruin everything.

She slipped her hand from his and rose from her seat. "I think I'd better check on the meal."

His chair scraped back as he stood. Always the gentleman. "Of course."

She scurried off, mentally kicking herself. An image of Adam's disappointed face followed her into the kitchen.

Three

"Damn it." Adam squeezed his eyes shut. He'd almost blown it with Mia. She was skittish, and he couldn't blame her. She didn't know him. It had been his MO not to let people in, and he'd done a good job of avoiding her questions tonight. He'd lost the fine art of conversation years ago, if he'd ever had it. If only he wasn't so darn smitten with her. *Smitten?* Now that was a corny word. Hell, he was attracted to her, big-time. She was a breath of fresh air in his stale life.

He entered the kitchen holding two wineglasses he'd refilled and found her by the oven, wearing her little blue apron again. His throat tightened at the domestic scene. How long had it been since a woman cooked him a meal? Well, aside from Mary. A long, he couldn't remember how long, time. "Me again." He set down her wineglass. "What can I do?"

"How are you at making a salad?"

"I can manage that."

She stirred the sauce as he opened the refrigerator and grabbed a big wooden bowl covered with plastic wrap. He set it in front of her.

"How's this?"

"Looks beautiful." She smirked. "You work fast."

"Thank Mary. She anticipates everything." He opened a drawer and revealed a loaf of fresh crusty Italian bread. "Yep, even bread."

Mia smiled. "Thank you, Mary. The sauce is almost ready. I brought homemade tagliatelle. But I can't take credit for making it. There's no way I could duplicate my gram's recipe. She's the expert. She made it."

Several sheets of thin pasta were laid out on a chopping block. Mia rolled a sheet all the way up until it was one rather long log and then she cut inch wide strips and then narrower strips all the way down the line. "Tagliatelle doesn't have to be perfect. That's the beauty in the recipe. Once you've made the pasta, cutting it is a breeze." She unrolled two at different lengths and widths and showed it to him. "See?"

She added a sprinkling of salt to a boiling pot. "Here you go. Want to put these in as I cut?"

"I think you can double as a chef, Mia D'Angelo." They worked together, her cutting, him adding the pasta to the bubbling water.

"That's nice of you to say. But judge me in two minutes, when it's done."

"If it tastes anything like it smells…" The scent of garlic and herbs and the meaty sauce spiked his appetite. The homey aroma brought good memories of sitting down to a meal with his mom and dad, brother and sister. "It'll be delicious."

"I hope so."

He helped Mia serve up the dish, and they sat down outside again. It was dark now; the moonlight over the ocean illuminated the sky. Mary had placed domed votive candles on the table, and he lit them. He couldn't remember having a more relaxed evening. Mia didn't seem to want anything from him. She was the real deal, a woman he wouldn't have even met, if she hadn't injured herself practically on his doorstep. She was curious, but she wasn't overbearing. He liked that she made him laugh.

Steam billowed from the pasta on his plate and he hunkered down and forked it into his mouth before his stomach started grumbling. The Bolognese sauce was the best he'd ever tasted, and the pasta was so tender, it slid down his throat. The dish was sweet and savory at the same time, just the right amount of…everything. "Wow," he said. "It's pretty damn good."

She grinned. "Good? Your plate is almost empty."

"All right. It's fantastic. I'm going in for second helpings. If that's okay with you?"

"If you didn't, I'd be insulted." She ladled another portion of pasta onto his plate and grated parmesan cheese in a snowy mound over it. "There—that should keep you happy for a while."

"I'll have to double my swim time tomorrow."

"How long are you out there usually?"

"I go about three miles."

"Every day?"

He nodded. "Every day that I'm home."

She swirled pasta around her fork. "Do you travel much?"

"Only when I have to. I'm doing a big job right now on the coast of Spain. It might require some traveling soon."

"I'd love to travel more. I rarely get out of California. Well, there was this one trip to Cabo San Lucas when I graduated high school. And my father's family was from West Virginia. I spent a few weeks there one summer. But oh, your life sounds so exciting."

It wasn't. He didn't enjoy traveling. He liked the work, though, and it was necessary to travel at times. Adam pictured Mia on the southern coast of Spain with him, keeping him company, lounging in a villa and waiting for him to return home from work. He saw it all so clearly in his mind that he missed her last comment. He blinked when he realized he'd been rude. "I'm sorry—what did you say?"

"Oh, just that I've always wanted to see Italy. It's a dream of mine, to see where my mother's family was from. That's all."

He nodded. Many people would love to trace their roots, but if Adam never entered the state of Oklahoma again, he wouldn't miss it. Not in the least. After Lily died, their family had never been the same. Some nights he woke up in a sweat, dreaming about the natural disaster that had claimed his sister's life. "I can understand that. Italy is a beautiful country."

"Have you been there?"

"Once, yes."

She took a long sip of wine. His gaze was riveted to her delicate throat and the way she took soft swallows. He didn't want the evening to end. If he had his choice, she'd be staying the night, but that would have to wait. Mia couldn't be rushed, and he wasn't one to push a woman into something she wasn't ready for. "After dessert, would you like to take a walk on the beach? I promise I'll bring a flashlight, and we'll be careful."

Mia turned her wrist and glanced at the sparkly silver bracelet watch on her arm. "I would love to, but it's getting late. Maybe just dessert this time. But I'll take a rain check on that walk."

Late? It was a little after ten. "You got it. Another time then."

They brought the dishes inside and Adam pulled out a strawberry pie from the refrigerator. "Mary brought this over this morning. That woman is a saint. I gave her the day off, yet she still came over with this pie."

Fresh whipped cream and split strawberries circled the top of the pie.

Mia took a look. "Wow, it's beautiful. Mary reminds me of my gram. Eating is a priority. And she makes enough food for an army. You'll never go hungry if my gram is around."

"I think I like her already." Adam grabbed a cake knife from the block.

"You would. She's the best."

Adam made the first cut, slicing up a large wedge of pie. "Whoa," Mia said, moving close to him. "I hope that piece is for you."

Her hand slid over his as she helped guide the knife down to cut another thinner wedge. Instant jolts hit him in the gut. Mia touching him, the softness of her flesh on his. She'd gotten under his skin so fast, so easily. Her scent, something light, flowery and erotic, swam in his head, and he couldn't let her go.

"Mia," he said. Turning to her, the back side of his hand brushed a few strands of hair off her face. Her eyes lifted, jade pools glowing up at him. They both dropped the knife, and he entwined their fingers, tugging her closer until her breasts crushed against his chest. "Mia," he said again, brushing his mouth to her hair, her forehead and then down to her mouth. His lips trembled there, waiting for invitation.

"Kiss me, Adam," she whispered.

His mouth claimed hers then, tenderly, a testing and tasting of lips. Oh God, she was soft and supple and so damn tempting. He was holding back, not to frighten her, holding back to give her time to get used to him. Every nerve in his body tingled.

She touched his face, her fingertips tracing the line of his jaw. A sound emerged from his throat, raw and guttural, and as her willing lips opened, he drove his tongue into her mouth. Her breath was coming fast—he could feel it, the rapid rise and fall of her breasts against his chest. His groin tightened, and he fought for control. He had to end the kiss. Had to step away. She turned his nerves into a crazed batch of male hormones. He swept his tongue into her soft hollows one more time, then mastered half a step back, breaking off the connection.

It was too much, too soon and crazy. She brought out his primal instincts. The jackhammering in his chest heated his blood. He held her in his arms, his forehead pressed to hers; then he brushed a kiss there. "Go out with me tomorrow night, Mia," he whispered. There was raw urgency in his request. Did he sound desperate?

Her expression shifted from glazed-over passion to concentration. Her silence worried the hell out of him. "Okay," she finally whispered back, her voice breathy and as tortured as his. "I'd better go now, Adam."

He didn't want her to leave. He couldn't get enough of her, but he wasn't going to press his luck. She wasn't a one-night-stand type of woman, and he was glad about that. "I'll see you out." He took her hand, the strawberry pie forgotten, and walked her to the front door. Rubbing the back of his neck, he gazed into her eyes. "Thanks for the meal."

"My pleasure."

"It was delicious." So was she. "I'll need your address."

"Six four, six four Atlantic. It's easy. Apartment ten, first floor."

He repeated her address, cementing it into his brain, and then opened the door for her. "I'll walk you to your car."

It was only a few steps, but he took her hand again, fitting it to his and she turned her leaf-green eyes his way. He melted a little inside. It would be a long twenty hours. "I'll pick you up at seven?"

"That's perfect."

Breath released from his lungs. "See you then."

He bent his head and placed a chaste kiss on her lips. Her sweet taste and softness seared him like a sizzling-hot branding iron.

He shut her car door. As she started the engine he gave her a smile, lifting his hand in a wave. Mia wiggled her fingers back and drove down his driveway, turning onto Pacific Coast Highway.

He stood rooted to the spot, breathless.
Mia D'Angelo had literally stumbled into his life.
What kind of fantastic dumb luck was that?

Four

"It's gonna cost you, Mia." She glanced in the ladies' room mirror of the nightclub, frowning at the reflection staring back at her. She was going to tell Adam the truth, sometime tonight during their date. She couldn't put it off any longer. Deep down in her heart, she knew Adam Chase was a decent man. She could feel it in her bones. She'd had a few boyfriends who'd been bad mistakes. Boyfriends who had cheated on her or given her a sob story every time they ran out of cash. How many times had she dipped into her own pocket to lend them a hand only to be taken advantage of again?

She wasn't that naive woman any longer. She'd learned from her mistakes, especially after she'd been burned by a master, her dear old dad, who was a terrible father and an even worse husband. He'd cheated on her mom and done much worse. A drunk and a womanizer, he'd brought shame and heartbreak to the family. He'd taken a life, running down an innocent young girl while under the influence. Gin was his poison of choice, and he'd reeked of it when he'd been hauled off to jail.

But Adam Chase, swimmer, rescuer, talented architect, wasn't a mistake. It was a feeling she got every time she was with him. Even though trying to delve into his past to learn more about him proved fruitless—the guy didn't like talking about himself—Mia owed it to Rose and to Adam to reveal her secret.

It had been on the tip of her tongue to reveal the truth a couple of times tonight. Once, just as she was about to say something, the waiter had come by with their meal and she'd lost her nerve. And later, as she was about to speak up again, the band had kicked up, drowning out her thoughts. Adam had asked her to dance then, and she couldn't refuse those expectant eyes gleaming at her. She'd taken his hand and danced close to him, losing herself in the music. Losing herself in him.

Now she had no excuse. She was going to march right out here, sit down next to him and ask for his patience and understanding. This was it. The time for stalling was over. This was going to be the hardest thing she'd ever had to do in her life. Tears stung her eyes and threatened to ruin her mascara. She dabbed at them with a tissue, took a breath and bucked up.

Her high heels clicked against the wood floors like a death march as she made her way back. The room was dark, the blues music in tune with her edgy mood. Keeping her eyes averted, unable to look Adam in the eye, she reached their table. Her mouth dropped open and she quickly clamped it shut. Sitting next to her date was none other than Dylan McKay.

Movie star. Sexiest man of the year. Box office gold. So much for her well-rehearsed confession. Her mind fuzzed over. She was looking at Hollywood royalty.

Both men instantly rose to their feet. "Mia D'Angelo," Adam said. "I'd like you to meet my neighbor Dylan."

"Hi, Mia." He extended his hand.

"Hello." She placed her hand in his and smiled casually as if she met megastars every day of the week. "Nice to meet you."

"Same here. I have to say I'm impressed. Not too many people can get Adam out of the house. Lord knows, I've tried a hundred times."

Adam shot him a glare. "Give it a rest, McKay."

Dylan flashed a brilliant ultrawhite smile, mischief playing in his eyes. "Adam and I have been neighbors for a few years now. He keeps to himself, but he's a good guy." Dylan winked, and Adam seemed to suffer through it. It was hard not to smile, Dylan was a charmer. Gosh, she'd seen every one of his films. Dylan pulled out the seat for her before Adam could get to it. She caught him frowning.

"Thank you," she said. She lowered herself down, and he scooted the chair in.

"Don't you have to be going?" Adam remarked, giving Dylan McKay some sort of male signal with his eyes. Mia stifled a chuckle.

"Yes, actually. I have a hot date with an older woman. She loves jazz."

Adam's brows shot up. And then he seemed to catch on. "Your mom's visiting?"

Dylan nodded. "She loves jazz. She brought my little sis with her this time. I'd bring them over, but I don't want to bust in on your date."

"The way you did?" Adam said drily, taking his seat.

Dylan didn't take offense. "Hey, I didn't want to be rude and not say hello." Dylan bent over to Mia, and she peered directly into his clear blue eyes. "Are you Italian?"

She nodded. "My family's from Tuscany."

"It's a beautiful country. I want to do another film there, just to absorb the culture and the food. Have you ever been?"

"No, it's a dream of mine to go one day. My gram tells some great stories of the old country."

"You'll get there. Nice meeting you, Mia. Adam. Have a nice evening, you two."

"Thanks." Adam rose to shake his hand. They seemed to have an easy friendship.

As he took his seat, Adam said, "Well, now that Dylan gave me his seal of approval as a nice guy, will you dance with me again?"

He was already rising, taking her hand and piercing her with those sharp metallic eyes. A soft, sultry, bluesy tune whispered over the conversational hum of the nightclub. He tugged her to the middle of the dance floor and brought her in close, folding her hand in his and placing it on his chest. "Thank you for not going all fan-crush crazy for Dylan. His ego's big enough."

"He came across very down-to-earth."

"He's easy with people. That's probably why he's loved by the masses."

Adam was the exact opposite of Dylan, quiet and closed off. For all she knew, the only thing they had in common was that they both lived on Moonlight Beach, and were probably billionaires or close to it. "You like him."

Adam gave a short nod. "He's a good friend." He tightened his grip on her and whispered, "Are you enjoying yourself tonight?"

"Very much."

Adam brushed a soft kiss to her hair, and she melted into him. "So am I," he whispered into her ear.

As they danced silently, his heartbeat echoed into her chest. Feeling the music, moving to the rhythms, the saxophone delivering gloriously soulful notes, she was floating on air. When the music stopped, Adam didn't move. He pushed a strand of hair from her face, gazing at her as if she was made of something precious and fine. Then he touched his mouth to hers, a tender claiming of her lips that stole her breath. His hands roamed over her partially backless dress possessively; her skin tingled where his fingers touched her skin.

His breath hitched, a small guttural sound emanating from his throat, as he continued to kiss her. Luckily, they were still ensconced on the crowded dance floor with couples waiting for the next song to begin. When the music started up again, he tugged her off the floor and they returned to their table, but he didn't sit down. Instead he took her face in his palms, gave her another wonderful kiss and gazed deeply into her eyes. "Mia, I have to get you home."

Why? Would he turn into a pumpkin at the stroke of midnight? But then he inched closer. Restraint pulled his face tight, his eyes pleading, and she instantly understood why he needed to get out of the nightclub.

She nodded, a beam of hot tingling heat spreading through her body. "I'm ready."

The courtyard near her apartment was dimly lit. Rays of moonlight reflected off a pond and flowed over the hibiscus bushes by her front door. "Thank you for a lovely evening," she said, turning to Adam. He let go of the hand he held and mumbled something she didn't quite hear. Her brain had scrambled during the limo ride home between bouts of sensual caresses and kisses that sent her soaring into the stratosphere.

She'd lost her nerve, once again. And she vowed, tomorrow, after all this heat and energy died down, she'd meet with him on neutral turf and tell him the truth.

"I'm sorry—what did you say?" she asked.

He braced his arms against the front door and trapped her into his body's embrace. His scent, a hint of lime and musk emanating from his pores, did wild things to her. Her thoughts, her body, were keyed into him. Below her belly, she ached and tingled, the pressure building. Her breasts pressed the boundaries of decency and the pebbly tips jutted out, stretching the material of her dress.

"Invite me in, Mia."

And then his lips were on hers again, taking her in another mind-numbing kiss. Her soul was seared, branded by a man she hardly knew. Yet it felt right. So very right. How could she be so attracted to the same man her sister had slept with? Conceived a baby with? This wasn't going to happen. It couldn't.

Her little plan was backfiring.

Because as much as the battle raged inside her head with all those thoughts, she couldn't stop kissing Adam. She couldn't stop wanting him. She hadn't yet said yes or no, and his kisses kept coming, delving and probing her mouth, his lips teasing and tempting hers. She tingled and ached for him, and when he placed the flat of his palm across her chest, rubbing at the sensitive tip through her clothes, a flood of warmth pooled down below, and a strangled sound rose from her throat. "Adam."

She was breathless, out of oxygen and falling fast.

He was an amazing kisser.

He was probably an amazing lover.

How long had it been since she'd been flipped inside out like this?

Maybe never.

She slipped a hand into her beaded purse, grabbed for her key and pressed it into his hand. "You're invited in," she said, her voice a raspy whisper.

"Thank God." Adam blew out a relieved breath.

She moved slightly away from the wall, her body ragged and limp already, just from his kisses.

A thought scurried into her mind of the baby's gear. *Oh no!* Was it all tucked away? Mentally picturing each room, she summed up that the coast was clear. For now, and that was all that mattered.

She didn't want to think further than this moment. She couldn't refuse Adam anything. In seconds, she was inside her apartment, deep in his embrace.

If she expected him to rip at her clothes, he didn't. He took her hand in his and brushed a soft caress to her mouth. More deliberately now, he spoke over her lips. "This is crazy. I don't want to rush you, Mia."

Adam, always rational. She was beginning to understand that about him. Even in the heat of passion, he thought of her feelings. His eyes were hot embers, his body on fire, yet he slowed down enough to make sure he wasn't taking advantage of her or the situation. "I don't feel rushed, Adam." Her voice softened as she confessed the truth.

He drew breath into his lungs as if he'd prayed for that answer and nodded.

She pushed his dinner jacket off his shoulders and he wiggled out of it. He wore no tie, but he unfastened the top buttons on his shirt. She took his hand and led him to the sofa. He sat first and tugged her down onto his lap. "You're beautiful." The heat in his eyes bored straight into her, and then his lips were on her again, his tongue mating with hers.

She gripped his shoulders, touched his hot sizzling skin from beneath his shirt. His strength rippled through her body and heightened her thrill. A low guttural growl rose up from his throat and touched something deep and tender in her heart. Nothing else existed in the world. It was all Adam. Adam. Adam.

He lowered her down slightly, holding her by one strong arm as the heat of his palm covered her breast. It swelled even more, aching for his touch. It was easy for him to slip down the one shoulder strap of her dress. The material and her strapless bra edged down; cool air hit her exposed chest. She arched for him, and he bent his head, taking her into his mouth.

She moaned as he suckled gently, his tongue moistening her extended nipples. Mia wiggled, and he held her arms firm, stroking her over and over, torturing her with swipes that left her breathless. The apex of her legs began to throb, a deep building of pressure that would soon need release.

His mouth left her breast then to reclaim her lips. The hem of her dress was pushed up and the rough planes of his hand cupped her leg, skimming the underside of her thigh, back and forth.

Her mind swam with delicious thoughts as pressure climbed. His fingertips came close to her sweet spot, and she ached for his touch.

"You want this, right?" he rasped, his fingers teasing closer.

"Yes," she breathed, her pulse racing. "I want it."

It wouldn't take much to send her over the edge. She was almost there already. She'd never been so in tune with a man before. She'd never had this kind of immediate response. And she wasn't ashamed that she was practically begging him to take her.

His fingers slipped beneath her bikini panties, and his touch brought a sudden sharp breath from her lips. "Easy, sweetheart. I won't hurt you."

She nodded, unable to utter a word.

As he moved over her, moisture coated his fingers, and, ever so slightly, her body began to rock and sway as he stroked her. Sensations swirled, and she gave herself up to the wondrous feeling. Adam's mouth on hers, his tongue inside her and his fingers working magic—she was too far gone to hold back. She let go and moved with him now. He pressed her harder, faster and she climbed as high as she could go.

"Mia." His voice tight, he seemed just as consumed as she was.

Her body gave way, releasing the strain, the heavy weight loosening up and shattering. Her eyes closed, she merely allowed herself to feel. And it felt mind-blowingly wonderful.

She opened her eyes to Adam's stare. The hunger on his face told her he was ready for more.

He brought down the hem of her dress and replaced the strap over her shoulder. She was being lifted again, tucked into his arms. Kissing her throat, he whispered, "Where's your bedroom, sweetheart?"

She pointed toward the darkened hallway. "The last door on the left."

He began to move slowly, cradling her. "Are you okay?"

She gave a slow nod. "I'm perfect." There was no shame.

She couldn't wait to be with him again, to have him inside her. She was just getting started. How many years had she gone without? Now, having Adam as a partner, her bones jumped to life.

"I agree. You are."

The compliment seeped into her soul.

He walked past Rose's bedroom. The door was shut, hiding her nursery, but a jolt of guilt-ridden pain singed her. She didn't want to think about that right now. Things were getting complicated.

They neared her bedroom door.

And then she was nearly falling out of his arms.

He tripped, and she went down with him. The stumble brought him to his knees. He never let go of her, though—good lifeguarding skills—and he laughed in her ear. "I've still got you. Sorry for the stumble. I must've stepped on something."

He set her down gently and searched the floor, picking up the mystery item that caused the fall.

Her eyes squeezed shut.

"What the hell is this?"

He groped at the stuffed snowman with the giant carrot nose. Olaf, the character from *Frozen*. She remembered Rose dropping it as she was getting ready to go to her grandmother's house. She'd meant to grab it but had totally forgotten.

"It's a toy I forgot to pick up."

"Do you moonlight as a babysitter or something? Or do you have a thing for weird-looking snowmen?"

She sighed. Then stood up and flipped the light switch on.

Adam squinted and gazed at her through narrowed eyes. "Mia? I was just kidding. Why are you frowning?"

Her heart sank, and tears burned behind her eyes. The night would bring on so many changes. Rose's innocent face flashed. For a split second, she thought about bailing. About lying to Adam and sending him packing. In her dreams, Rose was hers, Gram would live forever and they'd be a family.

"Mia?" Adam rose from the floor. She couldn't put this off any longer. It was time. She had the perfect opportunity to tell Adam about Rose. To lie now would only prolong the inevitable and make things harder than they already were.

"Adam, that's Olaf. It's, uh…it's your daughter's favorite toy."

It took all of her effort to get Adam to sit down at the kitchen table so she could explain. As she filled the coffeemaker, she sensed his gaze boring into her like a pinpointed laser beam and her neck prickled. He kept looking at her as if she were from outer space.

"This is some kind of joke, isn't it, Mia?"

"No joke. You have a daughter."

He shook his head. "I'm still waiting for your explanation. You can't just blurt out I've got a daughter and then decide we need to discuss this over coffee, as if we were talking about the weather. Christ, Mia. I've had people try to infiltrate my territory and invade my privacy. I admit you're good. You found a way to get my attention. Even it if did cost you pain and a little bleeding. Hell, you had me fooled. Whatever you want, just spill it out, so we can get this over with."

Her head whipped around, her eyes burning hot. "I'm not trying to fool you or invade your precious privacy, Adam. And you wouldn't say that if you knew Rose. That baby is the sweetest thing on this earth." She simmered down. She so didn't want to have a confrontation. "We need to discuss this calmly, rationally."

"How do you know I have a daughter? Who is she to you?"

"She's…my niece."

"Your niece?" His voice rose, piercing her ears. He hadn't expected that, but the truth deserved to be told now.

"Yes, my niece. About a year ago, you spent some time with my sister. Her name was Anna Burkel."

Adam frowned and darted his eyes away, as if trying to recall.

"She was dark blonde and pretty and, well, you spent one night with her."

Adam turned back to her and blinked. "She's your sister?"

Trembling, she poured coffee into mugs and brought them to the table in her small kitchen. Steam rose up and she stared at it a second. All of her mistakes came bounding back at her, and her hand shook as she set the mug down in front of him. "Yes, she was my sister."

"Was?"

"She died after giving birth to Rose. It was a complicated delivery."

Adam didn't offer condolences. He was in shock, staring at her face, but seeing straight through her. "Keep going, Mia. I'm not connecting the dots."

Her heart pounded. This wasn't going well. And it was probably going to get a lot worse. "I'll try to explain. When you met Anna, she was at a low point in her life. She was in love with Edward, her fiancé of two years. They had planned to get married that summer, but then Edward broke it off with her. I doubt she told you any of this, on… on that night."

He shook his head. "No, she didn't. I only remember that she looked lonely. I was at an art museum in the early hours, just when it opened," he said, gazing out the window to the dark sky. "I only make rare visits. But she was there, too, wandering around, and we were enthralled with the same piece. She said something that intrigued me about the artist. She seemed to know a lot about art. We had that in common. We struck up a conversation and ended up spending the day together. Are you saying she got pregnant that night?"

"Apparently."

"Apparently," he repeated. "Well, what is it Mia? Yes or no?" He rose from his seat and began pacing. "Are you trying to hustle me?"

"No! Damn it, Adam. I'm not doing that. And, yes, she got pregnant that night."

"So why didn't she try to find me and tell me about the baby?"

"Because she didn't tell anyone she was carrying your baby. She kept the secret from everyone, including her fiancé. She got back together with Edward just one month later and, and…" Oh, man, this was harder to admit than she'd thought. Saying the words out loud made her sister's deed seem conniving and sinister. What she'd done was wrong, and Mia had been shocked to learn the truth on Anna's deathbed. But how could she blame her sister now? She'd paid the worst price, dying before she got to know her sweet child.

"And she pretended that the kid was his?" Adam's lips twisted into a snarl. She didn't think his handsome face could ever appear ugly, but right now it did.

She nodded.

He stopped pacing and closed his eyes as if absorbing it all. "I'm not convinced the child is mine. How can you be so sure?"

"Because my sister was dying when she confided the truth to me, Adam."

"And?"

She bristled. "If that's not enough, Rose has your eyes."

"What does that mean?"

"How many children do you know have silver-gray eyes?"

"I don't know many children, Mia."

Now he was being obtuse. Yes, it was a lot to lay on him and she hadn't planned on his finding out this way… accidentally. It would've been much better if she could have confessed the truth to him during a long soulful talk, the way she'd hoped.

"How old is the baby?" he asked.

"Rose is four months."

His hands went to his hips. He might've been a gun-slinger, eyeing his opponent. He stood ramrod stiff and ready to do battle. "Four months? The child is four months old?" He paced again, moving briskly, and she imagined his head was ready to spout steam any second. "So what was all this about?" He gestured to her apartment, the couch where she'd come undone in his arms and all the rest, by making a circle with his hand. "Were you trying to soften the blow? Because, Mia, you're good. I'd say you're a pro."

The "pro" comment had her walking up to him, her nerves absolutely raw. "Don't insult me, Adam. Bullying doesn't work on me."

She'd been called many names in high school after her father had sullied the Burkel name. It had hurt her beyond belief. She'd felt dirty and shamed. Mean-spirited folks aimed their disgust and revulsion at her entire family, instead of the one person who'd actually been guilty of hideous crimes. James Burkel deserved their distrust, but not the rest of her family. They'd been innocent victims, as well.

From that day on, Mia had vowed not to allow anyone to bully her again.

"You sure had me fooled." And then Adam's eyes widened and he pointed a finger at her. "Did you plant that broken bottle on the beach, just to meet me?"

"Don't flatter yourself, Adam. I was trying to meet you, yes, that's true, but I wouldn't bloody myself. That was an accident."

"But it did the trick, didn't it?"

Oh man. She couldn't deny it. "Yes, it served my purpose."

"And that was to what? Screw me, as many ways as you could. And I'm not talking about sex, but honey, after tonight, if the shoe fits."

Fury blistered up and her hand lifted toward his face. He stared her down, and she dropped her hand, not because she was afraid of Adam, but because she didn't approve of physical violence of any kind. There had been one too many slaps to her mother's face by dear old dad for her to ever want to repeat that behavior.

He sensed her displeasure and backtracked a little. "I apologize for that. But just tell me why you waited for four months and why, when we first met, you didn't immediately tell me about Rose?"

"For one, my sister died before I could get much information out of her. She told me your name and that you were an architect. Do you know how many Adam Chases there are in the United States? Logic had me narrowing it down to a handful of men, but then I found a recent picture of you…which, by the way, wasn't easy to find. You're not exactly press happy, are you?" She didn't expect him to answer. It was common knowledge that he was a recluse, or whatever kind of label fit a man who didn't like people or being out in public. "When I saw a picture of you, and homed in on your eyes, well, then I knew it had to be you."

"What else?"

"Nothing else. Isn't that enough? I was right. You were with my sister."

"What about this Edward guy? Does he still believe the baby is his?"

An exhausted sigh blew through her lips. This had been a trying day, and her emotions were tied up into knots. "No, Anna left it up to me to tell him. He didn't believe me at first and I understood that. He didn't *want* to believe it. He had already bonded with Rose. When the DNA test came back, he was devastated. He'd lost Anna, and then to find out Rose wasn't his... I've been raising Rose ever since."

"Where is the baby now?"

"With my gram." Taking her eyes off Adam, she glanced at the wall clock. "I have to get her soon. She'll be fast asleep."

"I want to see her, Mia. Tomorrow morning. First thing." It was the first time Adam Chase barked an order at her.

"I'll have to make arrangements. I'm expected at work, but I'll be there."

"See that you are. Who watches the baby when you're working?"

"I do. She's too much for my gram all day. I take her to the shop, and she's pretty good. She takes naps. And some days I work part-time or work from home. She's my little mascot."

"You never explained why it took you so long to reveal this little secret. Why didn't you just come out and tell me about her?"

His eyes locked in on her, and it was clear he wouldn't let her off the hook. She could tell him she was charmed and mesmerized by him. But that would only compound the problem. Her palms began to sweat. "You're not going to like it."

"I've liked nothing about his evening, so why stop now?"

Ouch, another sharp blow. She felt something for Adam Chase, and it hadn't been one-sided. But that was beside the point. "Rose is precious to me. She's all I have left of my sister and she's an amazing, beautiful, smart baby. I'd die for her, Adam. I couldn't just turn her over to a stranger. I had to get to know you as a person."

"Those nosy questions you kept asking me."

She nodded. "But you gave nothing away about yourself. I mean, other than you're a brilliant architect and you're pretty handy with a first aid kit."

A low guttural laugh crept out of his mouth. The sound

made her skin crawl. "You've got to be kidding? You were judging me? If Rose is my baby, where do you come off not telling me immediately?"

She had to make him see her logic. Certainly, he wouldn't condemn her for her actions. He had to see she had the baby's welfare at heart. "It's only because I was trying to protect Rose. Think about it, Adam. All I knew about you is that you had a one-night stand with my sister. That doesn't make you father material. I had to make sure you weren't—"

"What? An ax murderer? A criminal?" Blood rose to his tanned cheeks.

She nodded slowly. "Well…maybe," she squeaked. "I had to know you weren't a jerk or a loser or something."

His eyes widened.

Stop talking now, Mia.

"So you made yourself my judge and jury? Did I pass your test? I must have…since you practically let me—" His eyes roamed over her disheveled dress. "Never mind." He pushed his fingers through his hair. "I can't believe this."

"I was going to tell you tonight. I had it all planned, but then we kept getting interrupted."

"If I hadn't stepped on that toy, I might never have learned the truth."

"That you have a daughter?"

"Whether this child is actually mine remains to be seen. I meant I would've never found out what a liar you are."

He grabbed his jacket from the sofa and strode toward the front door. Handling the knob, he stopped and stared at the door, refusing to look at her another second. "Bring her over in the morning. If you don't show, I'll come for her myself."

"We'll be there, Adam."

He walked out, and the sound of the door slamming made her embattled body jump.

So far her "daddy test" plan was an epic fail.

Five

Adam gazed out his bedroom window to view overcast morning skies. His eyes burned like the devil. He shut them and flopped back against his mattress. "Ow."

Hammers pounded away in his skull, but he'd have to ignore the rumble. He had more pressing things to think about than his hungover state. He'd had too much mind-numbing vodka last night. In just a few hours, he'd come face-to-face with Mia again. The conniver. The liar. The woman who'd deceived him for days. He'd let down his guard, just like he had with Jacqueline, and look how that had ended. He'd given her his heart and trust and shortly after, she'd broken it off with him, falling madly in love with his brother instead. Nice.

He pinched the bridge of his nose and filled his lungs with air.

And now Mia claimed he'd fathered her sister's child. He didn't trust Mia D'Angelo as far as he could toss her. But the baby was another matter. If she was his, he'd make things right. Last night, before he'd taken to drink, he'd put the wheels in motion to find out his legal rights in all this. And to find out who Mia really was.

He remembered more and more about the night he'd shared with Anna. It had been on the anniversary of his sister's death, some twenty years ago. He'd gone out, because staying in always made him think too hard about Lily and then the guilt would come. So he'd escaped to the museum and had met an equally lonely woman and they'd had a nice time. Nothing too earth-shattering, and, afterward, they'd both agreed it was best not to see each other again. No phone numbers were exchanged. They'd barely known each other's names. It had been an impetuous fling.

A knock at the door sounded loudly. "It's Mary. I brought you something to make you feel better."

"Come in." He sat up. His head was splitting like an ax to logs. The tomato drink flagged with a celery stem popped into his line of vision. "I thought you might need this."

How did she always know what he needed?

"I saw an empty Grey Goose bottle on the counter and figured this might be a welcome sight this morning."

"Thanks. It's exactly what I need."

She handed him the glass. "Bad night? Or an extremely good one?"

He took a sip. "Might be a little bit of both. Take a seat." He gestured to the chair by the window. "I have something to tell you. We're going to have two visitors today…"

Two hours later, Adam walked out of his bedroom showered and dressed in a pair of jeans and an aqua-blue polo shirt. He was too keyed up to eat breakfast and his head-shredding hangover didn't allow his usual morning swim. Instead, he grabbed a mug of coffee and wandered outside. He walked to the outer edge of his stone patio and gazed at the steady waves pounding the shore. He sipped coffee, staring out.

The last time he'd thought about fatherhood, he was getting ready to ask Jacqueline to marry him. He'd fallen hard for her and thought they were in tune with one another. So much so, he'd wanted to spend the rest of his life with her. But life never turned out as expected. He'd been shell-shocked when Jacqueline broke it off with him. Shortly after, he'd accidentally found out she'd fallen in love with Brandon.

There'd be no marriage. No family with Jacqueline for him.

As it turned out, Brandon hadn't lasted long with Jacqueline. She'd left him three years later, after a tumultuous relationship, and finally married a college professor. She was living a quiet life on the East Coast now. His mother had given him the scoop, though he kept telling her it wasn't any of his business anymore.

Now his every thought revolved around being a father. A chill ran down his spine thinking of all the ways his life would change after meeting Rose. But first and foremost, he had to find out if she was his daughter.

Mary's voice from behind startled him. "Adam, they're here."

He pivoted around to see Mia holding the baby in her arms. Behind them, long sheer drapes flapped gently in the breeze, fanning around them as if framing the Madonna and her child. He held his breath; his limbs locked in place. They both wore pink, Mia in a long flowery summer skirt and a pale blouse. The baby, wrapped in a lightweight blanket with only her face peeking out, had sandy-blond hair. That was all he could see of her as he stood a good distance away. Mia gazed at the child she held, her eyes filled with love and adoration, and the sight of her again packed a wallop to his gut. She didn't look like the conniving liar he'd pegged her for last night. But he wouldn't be fooled again. Too much was at stake.

This could be a scam. Mia could be a gold digger. Maybe she'd conjured up all of this after learning about the fling he'd had with her sister. The baby might be an innocent pawn in the sick game she was playing. *Remember that, Adam.*

His gaze went to Mary, standing near them, her hand on her heart, her light eyes tender on the baby. "I'll take it from here, Mary. Thanks."

"Yes, thank you, Mary." The women exchanged a glance. "She's precious."

"Yes, she is," Mia responded.

"I'll leave you two to talk it out."

Adam waited for Mary to leave. Then he set the coffee mug down and strode the long steps toward them. Mia cradled the baby possessively, holding her haughty chin up, suddenly defiant. What did she think he'd do, wrestle the baby out of her arms and banish her from his house forever?

He faced Mia and swiveled his head to see the baby's face. Soft gray eyes, circled with a hint of sky blue, looked up at him. Adam's heart lurched. Oh, God, she did have his eyes.

"This is Rose."

He nodded, his throat tight.

"She was born on May first."

Mia unfolded the blanket, showing him her chubby little body outfitted in a frilly cotton-candy-colored dress. Ruffles seemed to swallow her up. Her little shoes and socks matched her dress. "She weighed seven pounds, seven ounces. She's almost doubled her birth weight now."

"She's a beauty," he found himself saying. His child or not, he couldn't deny the truth. "Let's get her inside the house."

"Good idea. She's probably going to need a diaper change soon. She feels a little wet."

Adam gestured for her to go first. She stepped inside the kitchen. He pressed a button on the wall and the sliding doors glided shut. "Where do you want to change her?"

"Mary said she put her diaper bag in the living room."

"In here," he said and moved ahead of her.

She followed him down the hallway and into a room he barely used, filled with sofas, tables and artwork. A bank of French doors opened out in a semicircle to a view of the shoreline.

"Mary says I don't use this room enough," he muttered,

lifting the diaper bag overflowing with blankets, bottles, rattles and diapers. "All this stuff is hers?"

"That's only part of it."

Mia's lips twitched, not quite making it to a smile. Her eyes were swollen and her usual healthy-looking skin tone had turned to paler shades.

"Where do you want to change her?" asked Adam.

"On the floor always works. She's starting to roll and move a lot. It's safer for her than putting her on the sofa where she might topple. Hand me a diaper and a wipe out of there, please?"

Adam dug into the bag, pulling the items out, while she kneeled onto the floor, laid the baby's blanket down and then placed Rose on top of it. "That's right my little Sweet Cheeks—we're going to clean you right up."

The baby gave her a toothless grin and Adam had to smile. She was a charmer. Mia pressed a kiss to the top of her forehead. "Bloomers off first," she said, pushing them down beautifully chunky legs. "Now your diaper."

The baby kicked and cooed, turning her inquisitive little body to and fro. Something caught his eye on the back of her leg as the ruffles of her dress pulled up. A set of light brown markings, triangular in shape, stained her skin on her upper back thigh. Mia laid a hand on her stomach to hold her still while she cleaned the area with a diaper wipe. Adam kneeled down beside her to get a better look at that mark. He pointed to her thigh. "What's that on the back of her leg?"

Mia rolled the baby over ever so gently to show him. "This? It's nothing. The pediatrician said it's a birthmark. She said it'll fade in time and would be hardly noticeable."

Adam drew a deep breath. "I see."

The birthmark caught him by surprise. Up until now he hadn't been convinced about Rose's bloodlines. Gray-blue eyes were rare but not proof enough. But a family birthmark? Now that wasn't something he could ignore.

He'd been born with the exact marking in the same location, upper back thigh. Adam's father had had it, but as far as he knew, Lily and Brandon had escaped that particular branding. "I have the same birthmark, Mia."

Her eyes flickered.

"I still want a DNA test." His attorney had told him it was a must. For legal reasons, he needed medical proof. "But now I know for sure. Rose is my child."

The moment had finally come. Adam understood he was Rose's father. The birthmark she hadn't given a thought to had convinced Adam. Mia wanted this, but where did they go from here? How should they proceed? Adam hadn't said much of anything as to his plans. He'd asked countless questions about Rose, though. What was she like? Did she sleep through the night right away? Had she ever been ill? What foods did she like to eat?

Calmly and patiently she answered his questions as they sat on the sofa that faced the Pacific Ocean. Adam gawked as Mia fed the baby a bottle of formula.

He reached out to touch her hair, wrapping a finger around a blond curl. "She's been good, hasn't she?"

"She's usually very good. Not too many things upset her. She only makes a peep when she's tired. I rock her to sleep and that calms her."

"Do you sing to her?"

"I try. Thank goodness she's not a critic."

Adam laughed, a rich wholesome sound that would've had her smiling, if the situation was something to smile about.

"When she's done with her bottle, I'd like to hold her."

Mia drew breath into her lungs. The thought of handing her over to Adam, if only for a little while, turned her stomach. Soon she'd lose Rose to him forever. She had a right to see her from time to time, but it wouldn't be the same as raising her, day in and day out. Nothing would be the same.

Oh, how her heart ached. "Sure."

The baby slurped the last drops of formula, and Mia sat her on her lap and burped her, explaining to Adam how to do it in an upright position. The baby belched a good one, and she smiled. "That's my little trouper."

She hugged Rose to her chest, kissed her forehead and turned to Adam. "Are you ready?"

"Yes, but keep in mind, I haven't held a baby since my sister was born. And then I was only a kid."

"Just put your arms out, and let me give her to you."

He did just that, and she placed Rose into his arms. "She holds her head up now all by herself, but just make sure she doesn't wobble."

Mia positioned Adam's hand under the baby's neck and extended his fingers. Adam darted a glance at her. Their eyes connected for a second, and then he was focused back on the baby.

Rose squirmed in his arms, her face flushed tomato red. And then her mouth opened, and she let out an ear-piercing wail.

Adam snapped his head to her for help. "What do I do?"

"Try rocking her."

He did. It didn't help.

"What am I doing wrong?" he asked.

She didn't know. Usually Rose wasn't fussy. "Nothing. She doesn't know you."

Her wails grew louder and louder, and Mia's belly ached hearing her so unhappy.

"Maybe that's enough for right now," she said, reaching for the baby.

Adam was more than willing to give her back. "Hell, I don't know what I did to upset her."

"Please don't swear around the baby. And you did nothing wrong."

Mia put her onto her shoulder and rocked her. She stopped crying.

Adam shook his head. "Okay. What now?"

"Well, I'm due at First Clips in a little while. Rose and I should get going."

Adam's gaze touched upon the baby, a soft gleam shining in his eyes. He opened his mouth to say something, and then he clamped it shut. Was he going to refuse to let Rose leave? That could never happen. He wasn't properly equipped to have a baby here. And clearly he didn't know what to do with her. "I want to see her tomorrow. I want her to know me."

"I'll stop by again. Same time?"

He nodded and then helped her pack up the baby's stuff. He looked on fascinated as she strapped Rose into the car seat. "You'll have to teach me how to do that."

"It's not that hard." A man who designed state-of-the-art houses shouldn't find it a challenge to buckle a baby up. "Tomorrow, you'll fasten her in."

"All right."

She slung the shoulder bag over her shoulder and Adam lifted the bucket, walking her outside to her car. On the way out, little Rose peered up, watching him holding the handles of her car seat, and squawked out several complaints. Once at the car, they made an exchange. He took the diaper bag off her arms and she lifted the bucket onto its base and snapped it in, giving it a tug to make sure it was in tight. "There you go, little one."

"The baby rides backwards?" Adam asked.

"Until she's much older, yes."

He shrugged. "I guess there's a lot to learn."

"Tell me about it. I was petrified when I first took Rose home from Edward's house. It was a hard day for everyone."

Adam glanced at Rose again. Maybe he didn't have much sympathy for what she'd gone through, losing her sister, telling Edward the truth and then raising Rose these past months, but she'd done what she thought was right.

"I'll call you tonight," Adam said.

"Why?"

"She's my daughter, Mia. I've already missed enough time with her." There was no mistaking his condemning tone. He held her guilty as charged. "I want to know everything about her."

Yes, she was right. No sympathy.

She drove off his property as he stood in the driveway, hands in his pockets, watching her drive away and looking like he'd lost his best friend.

"Morning, Mia. Bad news. The rocket ship's on the fritz again." Sherry greeted her at the back entrance of First Clips and opened the screen door for her. Situated in the heart of the Third Street Promenade, the shop catered to an elite clientele of children from ages one to twelve years. "How about I watch the baby while you do your magic on that crazy machine."

Mia sighed. "I wish you and Rena would learn how to fix the darn thing. It's just a matter of replacing shorted fuses."

"I can calm a kid and cut hair on the wildest child, Mia, but you know I'm not good with mechanics. Luckily, our next client isn't due for another fifteen minutes. And she'll be sitting on the princess throne."

Baby Rose loved to watch the lights flicker on and off on the First Starship seat but she also loved the shiny tiaras and lighted wands the girls played with while seated on the Princess Throne.

Mia handed Sherry the handle to the baby's car seat. "Here you go. Auntie Sherry will watch you while I make all the pretty lights work again."

"Hello there, Rosey Posey. How's my little angel today?"

Rose cooed at her aunt Sherry. Today Sherry wore a

carnation-pink chambermaid costume with white ruffle sleeves. Her thick blond hair was up in a fancy do and she looked fit to coif the hair of the finest royalty. Sherry was a stylist extraordinaire.

Mia set about fixing the dashboard on the rocket ship. It took her all of five minutes to replace the fuses, and when the mission was accomplished she found Sherry rocking Rose to sleep in her office, which doubled as the baby's nursery. "Shh…she's out," Sherry whispered. "Sweet little thing." Sherry lowered her into the playpen as Mia looked on.

Sherry and Mia strolled into a small lounge that consisted of a cushy leather sofa and a counter with a coffee machine on top and a small refrigerator underneath.

"She's such a doll," Sherry said.

Mia smiled, grabbing two mugs and setting them out. "For everyone but her father." Steam rose up as she poured the coffee. She handed Sherry a cup, took her own and they both sat down. They held their mugs in their laps.

"Still? It's been how many days?"

"Today makes four. She's not warming to him, and I think he's really frustrated. He thinks if she sees him for more than an hour or two, she'll get used to him. And he has to get used to her, too. He's very unsure when he's holding her."

"It doesn't seem like a wealthy guy like that would be unsure of anything."

Mia sipped her coffee. "Babies are in a category all their own. They throw most men off-kilter. Doesn't matter how powerful or rich they are, there's something about babies that frighten them. They think of them as fragile little creatures."

"My brother has a six-month rule," Sherry said. "He won't hold a baby until they're sturdy little beings."

"What about little Beau? Did he back off from holding his own son?"

"He made an exception for Beau, but he still waited a good couple of weeks before he held him."

"Wow."

"I know. Me? I couldn't wait to get my hands on Beau. And you know how I feel about Rose. I love her like she's my own niece."

"I know, Sherry. She loves you, too. You're her auntie Sherry."

"I love that. So what about Adam?"

"What do you mean?"

"Well, you said he doesn't venture out much, he's sort of a recluse and he's got his head stuck in a computer all day. So, is he a geek?"

A sound rumbled up from her chest. "Not at all."

An image of Adam striding out of the ocean, toned and tanned, shoulders broad, arms powerful, beads of water sliding down his body as he made his way to her, wouldn't leave her head alone.

Rena stepped into the room wearing a metallic silver jumpsuit with triangular collar flaps. She was the First Starship captain. "Oh I came just in time." She poured herself a cup of coffee. "Tell us more about Adam."

"You know all there is to tell," Mia said. "As soon as he found out who I really was, he turned off completely. Shut me down. He's only interested in Rose. And right now she's not cooperating with him. It's sort of sad, seeing the disappointment in his eyes every time we leave."

"Turned off, completely? Does that mean he was turned *on* at one point?" Sherry asked.

Mia rubbed at the corner of her eyes, stretching the skin to her temples. She hadn't told her friends about her dates with Adam or the kisses they'd shared. Or the way he'd made her come undone on her living room sofa that night. It seemed like eons and not days ago since that happened. She couldn't tell Gram the details of what had transpired with Adam that night. Goodness no. "Well, maybe. As I told you before, we spent some time together. I was trying to get to know what kind of person he was and, yes, judging him to see if he was worthy of Rose."

"You had every right," Sherry said.

"You couldn't just drop her off and hope for the best," Rena said.

"Thanks for the support. It means the world to me, but, unfortunately, Adam doesn't see it that way. And well, I thought we might have had something pretty special."

Two sets of eyes pierced her, waiting for juicy news.

She went on. "Let's just say on a scale of one to ten, our date was an eleven. I know enough to believe it wasn't one-sided. He is very charming when he lets down his guard."

"You didn't tell us you went on a date!" Rena said.

"Was it flowers and chocolates?" Sherry asked.

"More like an amazing dinner and lots of dancing," she explained.

"Holding tight. Whispers in the ear?" Rena asked.

Mia nodded.

"And good-night kisses?"

"Oh yes, delicious good-night kisses."

"Mia, did you do it with him?" Sherry asked, darting a bright-eyed glance at Rena.

"Of course not." But almost, she wanted to add. Something made her hold that part back. She wasn't ready to tell them she'd come close to giving Adam her heart and her body that night. She'd lost her head and been fully consumed with passion. Had it been desperation that drove her or something else?

Their shoulders slumped; the fire in their eyes snuffed out. Her love life disappointed her friends. Oh well, what could she say? It disappointed her, too.

"He's filthy rich," Rena said.

"And rock-star handsome," Sherry added. "We wouldn't blame you."

"Or judge you," Rena said. "You've had it rough lately."

"You guys are the best. But he's Rose's father. And I have to watch my step from now on. Her future is on the line. That's all that matters to me right now."

"You're late." Adam grumbled, opening her car door for her.

His *pleasant* greeting grated on her already shot nerves. "Only by fifteen minutes. It's Friday night. There was a ton of traffic on the PCH." She climbed out of the driver's seat, taking the diaper bag with her.

Adam scratched his head. "If you'd let me have a car pick you up, we wouldn't run into this problem."

"Adam, we've been over this. Does your car drive *over* traffic? Because if you had one that did, I'm sure it would replace the Rolls in your gallery."

Adam's mouth clamped shut. A tic worked at his jaw. He didn't like her attitude? Well, she wasn't crazy about his. This was her third stop today. She'd worked long hours, then rushed out of the salon just so she could get here on time. She'd hit bad traffic, which was no joy. And when she'd pulled up to his house, he was waiting for her outside like an irate parent, his displeasure written on the tight planes of his face. Where was that beautiful man she'd met on the beach?

"Come inside," he said.

He reached for the handle of the baby seat but thought better of it. Rose was awake, her gaze glued to his. One false move could start her on a crying jag. Once again, disappointment touched his eyes as he took the diaper bag off her shoulder and grabbed her purse. She followed him inside to the living area. It was after six, a beautiful time of day at the beach. The sun was fading and a glow of low burning light flowed in through the bank of opened French doors. A slight breeze blew into the room, ruffling the leaves on the indoor plants.

"If it's cold for the baby, I can shut the doors."

"No, this is fine. She's been inside all day. She could use a little air." And so could she. Her nerves were frazzled and the temperature was just right to cool off her rising impatience with Adam.

Once they were situated, Mia unfastened Rose from her restraints and picked her up. "There we go, Sweet Cheeks." Mia kissed both of the baby's cheeks, and Rose opened her mouth to form a wide toothless smile. Then she propped the baby on her lap and cradled her in the crook of her elbow.

Adam looked on. Longing was etched on his perfect features, and a twinge of guilt and sorrow touched her heart. He wanted to bond with Rose so badly, and she was having none of it.

"I'd like to hold her," Adam said.

"Okay. Come sit down next to me first."

He did. The scent of him—sand and surf and musk—packed a wallop. He was a towering presence beside her. If only she wasn't so darn attracted to him. "Let's give her a few minutes."

"Okay."

"Talk to me. Let her get used to the sound of your voice again." They'd done this before, and it hadn't worked. Maybe tonight it would make a difference.

"What would you like to know?"

"Everything. But you can start by telling me how your day went."

Adam hesitated. His face was pinched tight. She pictured the debate going on in his head before he finally agreed to open up. "Well, I took my usual swim this morning, after you left."

"Don't you swim just after dawn?"

"I'm a stickler about that, yes. But I woke up later than usual today and I didn't want to miss seeing Rose."

"How far did you swim this morning?"

He glanced at the baby. Rose's eyes were intent on him. It was uncanny how she measured him.

"Four miles."

"Four? I thought you usually did about three?"

"I, uh, had a little more energy to work off this morning."

"Why?"

He glanced at Rose.

"Oh." Rose had been unusually clingy and wouldn't let Adam get anywhere near her.

He didn't say more. "So then, what did you do after your swim?"

He lifted his head and stroked his chin thoughtfully. "My mother called."

"How nice. Do you speak with her often?"

"About once a week. It was a short conversation."

How she missed her own mother and the conversations they used to have. With Anna and her mother gone, she had only Gram. Her grandmother was wonderful, and Rose's arrival had given Mia's life more purpose.

"After that it was business as usual. I did some drafting, took a few calls. Went into the office for a few hours and got home in time to meet you."

"You didn't hesitate to scold me about being late."

Adam shot her a glance, bounded up from the sofa and walked over to the French doors, running his hands through his hair. Turning to her, his eyes were two tormented storm clouds. "Look, I'm sorry about that. I was worried about her. Do you have any idea how much I want to be a part of her life? I've already missed her first four months. I don't want to miss any more time with her."

She nodded. "Okay. I can understand that."

"Well, that makes me feel a whole lot better that you understand I want to know my daughter. I want to love and protect her."

"Adam."

"Let me hold her, Mia."

"Let's play a game with her first. She loves peekaboo. It might make her warm up to you."

"All right, fine." He softened his tone. "How do we do that?"

"I'll show you." She laid the baby down on a blanket on the floor. "Want to play peekaboo, Sweet Cheeks?" Rose's eyes followed her movement as if anticipating something more fun than a diaper change. "Come down here with me, Adam."

Adam scooted next to her, his thigh brushing hers as he positioned himself. Her body zinged immediately, which annoyed her. He didn't think much of her these days, and she should get the hint already. "Reach over to the bag and hand me a receiving blanket," she ordered.

Adam rummaged through her bag and came up with one. "This good?"

"Yes, thank you," she said and softened her tone. "Now watch."

Mia brought the blanket very close to Rose's face and left it there for three seconds so that she couldn't see them, and then quickly removed it. "Peekaboo!"

Rose broke out in cackles. It was the sweetest sound.

"See, she loves this game. Now you do it, Adam." She handed him the blanket.

"Okay, I'll give it a try. Here we go."

Adam repeated the same moves. "Peekaboo!"

Rose stared at him, her mouth curving up slightly, but no real smile emerged. Her legs were kick, kick, kicking. It was something she did when she was excited.

"Try it again. At least she's not crying."

"Okay."

He went through the peekaboo ritual again. The baby studied him. Her inquisitive eyes roamed over his face as if she couldn't quite figure him out. Mia felt like she had the same problem.

"I'm going to pick her up now," Adam said. He bent

and gently lifted her, cradling the back of her head and her buttocks. "That's it, little Rose," he said, carefully rising with her in his arms.

As if Rose finally realized what was happening, she turned abruptly in his arms, her body stretching out, stiffening up. Adam caught her before she wiggled free of his hold. She reached for Mia, her arms extended and pleading. Then she let out a scream.

Mia jumped up. "Rose!"

Adam held her back, firming up his grip. "Let me hold her, Mia. I'll walk her around and talk to her. She can't cry forever."

Mia bit her lip. Her stomach ached. It was torture hearing Rose cry and seeing her desperately reaching for her. "It might be longer than you think."

"Be positive, Mia. Isn't that what you tell me?"

"But she's crying for me."

"Maybe she wouldn't if she didn't see you. I'll take her in to see Mary."

He headed toward the kitchen, gently bouncing the baby in his arms. "Sing to her," she called to him. "She loves music."

Adam nodded and walked out of the room. She closed her eyes. But that only concentrated the baby's screeching cries over Adam's rendition of "Old McDonald Had a Farm." Her heart lurched, and she bit down on her lower lip to keep from calling to her.

She couldn't stand it.

She walked over to the French doors and stepped outside.

Mia sat across from a stony-faced Adam at the dinner table. Mary had left for the day, and Rose slept on her blankets on the floor of the living room. Mia pushed chicken Florentine around on her plate. Mary had outdone herself today with the meal, but Adam's quelling silence soured her stomach of any appetite she might've had.

He sipped wine, a fine Shiraz that went well with the meal. But Adam hadn't touched his food, either. He stared off, his gaze on the shoreline and the high tide rising. A gentle breeze blew by, coming in through the expanse of the open kitchen area, and she shuddered.

Adam glanced at her. She shook her head—she wasn't cold.

Not from the winds anyway.

"She wouldn't go to Mary, either," Adam said, mystified. "And Mary is good with children."

"I know. I heard Mary trying to calm her."

"She cried for twenty minutes in my arms. I tried everything."

He had. He'd sung out of tune to her. He'd bounced her. He'd taken her outside to see the beach. Then he'd sat down on a glider and swayed back and forth, trying to keep her from squirming out of his arms. Mia had hidden herself from the baby's sight and stolen quick glances. She couldn't help worrying over Rose. She'd taken care of her every need for four solid months. It had been a very hard twenty minutes, seeing the baby's anguish and knowing she needed her aunt Mia.

"She's too attached to you, Mia."

She jumped at his comment. "What does that mean?"

"It means that I want my daughter to know me. And that's not happening right now."

"Give it time, Adam."

"You keep saying that. How much time? The longer she's with you and you alone, the more attached she'll become. Isn't that obvious?"

"No, it's not obvious. She'll warm up to you. These are new surroundings, and she's only known you for a few days. She's fine with Rena and Sherry at the salon. She goes to them—so I know it's not just me she wants."

"Is it supposed to make me feel better knowing my daughter will go to perfect strangers, but she won't let her own father hold her, not even for a minute, without exercising her very healthy lungs?"

"Rena and Sherry are not perfect strangers. They are her family."

Adam's face reddened. "I'm her family, Mia."

Oh man. This evening wasn't going well. Her stomach lurched. Dread crept along her spine and knotted her nerves.

He bounded up and pushed his hands through his hair. He always did that when he was agitated. Several sandy-blond strands stood straight up, but Adam could get away with that look. It was appealing on him, a little muss to disrupt his perfectly groomed appearance.

"There's only one solution, Mia."

Her throat constricted. She buttoned her lips.

"Rose has to live here with me."

Oh God. Oh God. Oh God.

Her worst fears were coming true. She knew this day would eventually come, but hearing him say it ripped her apart. "No."

"No? Mia, she belongs with me. I've already missed so much time with her. Four months to be exact. I may not be a perfect father to her right now, but I've got to keep trying. I know if she's here, she'll come to accept me quicker. You can visit her any time you'd like. It's a promise."

Her eyes burned; the tears threatening to flow were white-hot flames. Her body shook, her lips quivering. "No, Adam. I can't leave her."

Adam watched her carefully. This was so hard. She tried to be brave, to put up a good front, but she was ready to fall apart. Any second now, she'd shatter into a mass of tears.

"I'll hire you on as a babysitter," he said, softer.

"A babysitter?" What was he saying? She sobered a little. Grabbing the table for support, she rose on wobbly legs. She couldn't sit still another second. "You want to pay me to take care of my beautiful niece? My own flesh and blood?"

"Hell Mia, do you have a better idea?"

"I already have a job, thank you very much. I own First Clips. I'm needed there."

His lips tightened to a thin line. His eyes became two stormy gray clouds. A battle seemed to rage inside his head. Seconds ticked by. Finally, he sighed as if he'd lost something treasured. "Fine, then. Just move in with me."

"M-move in with you? You couldn't possibly want that."

A wry laugh rumbled from his chest. "I don't see that I have a choice. If I want Rose here…"

"Then you're stuck with me, is that what you were going to say?"

"Don't put words in my mouth, Mia." He gave his head a shake. "You don't have any idea how important this is to me, or I wouldn't even consider inviting you into my home."

"But we'd be living together."

She caught his shudder. No, he didn't want this any more than she did.

"It's a big house," he countered, "and a solution to our problem. You both move in. You can come and go as you please, and I'll be able to see Rose whenever I want. She'll be here every day and night. And she'll come to accept me."

"I don't know," Mia said, stalling. The idea was sprung on her so quickly, she needed time to think it through.

"Mia, it's the only way to ease Rose into this transition more comfortably. It's best for her."

She didn't know if that was true. Adam wasn't thrilled with having her live with him. How could he be? It wasn't for romantic reasons. For all she knew, he hated her or at best resented her for the lies she'd told.

"I don't know if I can do it, Adam."

"And I don't see that we have any other choice. You want to be with Rose as much as I do."

"I know she's your daughter and you want to get to know her, but I don't understand why you are so insistent about this since you're clearly not comfortable around babies."

He stared at her, or rather, stared straight through her as if thinking hard about her question.

Finally, he sighed. "I have my reasons."

She shrugged, palms out gesturing to him for an answer.

"It's personal."

Of course. How could she believe he'd give her an upfront honest reason. That would mean he'd have to divulge something about himself.

She didn't see that she had any choice in the matter. "When and for how long?"

"Move in by the end of the week." He blinked, and then added, "We'll have to take it one day at a time from there."

She gulped.

"Just say yes, Mia."

It probably *was* the best solution for Rose. And Mia couldn't give her up cold turkey. She'd be getting what she ultimately wanted, a chance to keep Rose with her most of the time. Nothing would change other than her location. They'd just hang their hats at this gorgeous beach house instead of at her small apartment.

Her mouth opened and she heard a squeak come out. "Yes?"

Adam nodded, satisfied.

But just as he turned away, a shadow of fear entered his eyes.

The recluse's life was about to change dramatically.

And so was hers.

Six

The guest room on the second story of Adam's home was amazing. It wasn't cozy like her own bedroom, but she could certainly make do with the king-size bed, bulky light wood furniture and much more square footage than she'd need for her yoga workouts. There was a one-drawer desk by the window, a view of the ocean she couldn't complain about, a lovely white brick fireplace and a sixty-inch flat-screen television hanging on the wall. All her clothes would fit into two dresser drawers and one-tenth of the walk-in closet. Adam had let her choose her room and she'd chosen the one that suited her tastes the most. Namely, it was right next door to Rose's nursery.

"Oh listen, Rose. Hear the big trucks? They are coming with your brand-new furniture." Propped on pillows on the bed, Rose kicked her legs and watched her put her clothes away in the closet. The baby was learning how to roll, though she hadn't quite gotten the hang of it yet. Even so, Mia kept an eye on her every second. It was a long way down to the floor for a four-month-old.

Last night, Adam had enlisted her help in picking out nursery items the baby would need from a catalog, including a crib and dresser. Less than twenty-four hours later, they had arrived. Through the magic of…Chase money.

She sighed, although she was glad Adam insisted on buying Rose all new furniture. The baby deserved as much and it meant that Mia could keep Rose's nursery intact at her apartment for those times, if ever, she would take Rose there.

With a fold and a tuck, the last of her sweaters were stacked neatly into the dresser drawer. As she closed the drawer slowly with the flat of her hands, a shiver coursed through her body. Her future was uncertain. She'd been driven out of one home already. How long before Adam added to her pain? How long before she felt like that same unwanted, sullied guest that had overstayed her welcome and been asked to leave? And how could she leave Rose?

Grandma Tess hadn't taken the news lightly of Mia moving into Adam Chase's mansion. Mia had put a happy face on it, trying not to worry Gram with her own doubts. Gram didn't want her getting hurt. There'd been enough heartache in their family recently. Mia couldn't disagree. But she did point out the obvious. Adam was Rose's legal father—the DNA test results had come back positive—and he could provide Rose with a great future.

Sherry and Rena had a different opinion. They saw her move as an opportunity for Mia to spruce up her nonexistent love life. Mia had been dating the vice president of a financial firm six months ago, and her two pals had been sorely disappointed to learn that she'd broken it off with him weeks later. He'd been a player, fooling with women's hearts. Mia recognized the signs and the lies immediately. And she wanted none of those games. She'd seen what her mother had gone through, putting up with her father. Mia didn't want to make the same mistake. Rena and Sherry saw moving in with the mysterious, deadly handsome Adam Chase as a romantic adventure. Mia only saw it as a necessity. He'd given her no other option.

A sudden quiet knocking broke into her thoughts. She turned to the door she'd left partially open, and Adam popped his head inside. "How's it going?"

"We're doing fine. I'm just about unpacked."

Adam glanced at the baby on the bed. "May I come in?"

She nodded.

He took a few steps inside and gave the room a once-over, his gaze stopping on the items she'd put on the dresser—a framed photo of her mother and Gram in the early days and another of her holding the baby along with her gal pals at First Clips—then walked over to the bed, making eye contact with Rose.

She'd thought better of putting out Anna's picture right now, but she would eventually give it to Rose. The child had a right to know all about her mother.

"The movers are downstairs, ready to come up," he said, turning to her. "Would you mind showing them where you'd like everything to go?" He shrugged. "I haven't got a clue."

The irony hit her hard. The master designer needed help arranging baby furniture. "I can do that."

"Great."

Mia bent and gathered Rose into her arms. "Come on, Sweet Cheeks. We're gonna see your new digs."

Adam's lips twitched and a beam of love glistened in his eyes. He reached his hand out as if to stroke the baby's head, then retracted it quickly.

Mia pretended not to notice.

Thirty minutes later the movers were gone and the nursery was almost all set up. She sat on a glider, entertaining Rose with a game of patty-cake while Adam sat cross-legged on the floor staring at screws and nuts and wooden slats of the crib he'd laid out. "So you're telling me you put Rose's crib together all by yourself?" He spared her a glance over his shoulder.

"I sure did."

He scoured over the small-print instructions for all of ten seconds, his brows gathering. "I see."

"What?" she asked. "If a mere woman can do it, you should be able to knock it out without a problem?"

"I didn't say that," he said, his tone light.

She chuckled. "It was implied. I'm curious—why didn't you have the movers set it up?"

He swiveled around to face them, those gray eyes soft now on the baby. "It's the least I can do for Rose. A father usually sets up his baby's crib, doesn't he?"

A lump formed in her throat. Her heart grew suddenly heavy. The man who had everything wanted to do something meaningful for his child. "Y-yes. I suppose he does."

He nodded and turned back to his task.

"I'll put her sheets and towels into the wash," she said, rising. "They'll be ready for her tonight."

"Mary's got that covered."

"But does she have the right—"

"She raised three children," Adam said. "She knows all about laundering baby clothes."

"Oh, right. Okay."

"If you don't mind, I'd like you to stay in here until I get this thing put together."

"Don't mind at all. I can lend a hand if you get confused."

Adam turned to her. She grinned ear to ear and the frown on his face disappeared. Gosh, the man almost cracked a smile. "Smart aleck."

The house was finally quiet of noises that would fill his life from now on. Rose playing with her toys, Rose taking a bath, Rose crying for her bottle. Adam breathed a sigh of relief. This was his daughter's first official night in her home. He'd built the crib she was sleeping in now, his heart bursting as he looked at her small chest rising and falling with steady breaths.

Assembling the crib hadn't been too much of a challenge after all. His only struggle had been afterward, when he'd discovered eight leftover screws and bolts. He'd checked over the crib twice, pulling and tugging at it, testing the sturdy factor and only after Mia told him that the same thing had happened to her had he relaxed about it. The leftovers, she said, are either spares or a result of incompetence on the manufacturer's part. Either way, she'd given him her seal of approval on the crib.

And somehow, that had mattered to him.

Adam touched a small curl on Rose's head. If only he could bend over and kiss her sweet cheeks, wish her a good-night the way a father should. But he couldn't chance waking her and, worse yet, having her scream mercilessly at him.

She'd warm up to him. She had to. How long could he go without holding his own child?

He'd been given a second chance with Rose. He'd do better than he had with Lily. His sister had counted on him and when he'd let her down, it had cost her her life. That pain was always with him and drove him to the outskirts of life. He vowed solemnly not to ever let Rose down. Raising her, he'd try to make up for his failures with Lily and then maybe, he'd find a way to forgive himself.

Having Mia move into the house seemed like the only solution to keep Rose happy and content while living under his roof. For Rose's sake, he'd do anything to make up for lost time. Neither he nor Mia wanted it this way, but for all his business smarts and college degrees, he couldn't figure a way around it.

The architect couldn't draft a better design than the plan he'd come up with, so now he had two new females living under his roof.

Adam left his sleeping daughter and walked downstairs to the kitchen. Mary was long gone. She'd been smitten by Rose and had stayed longer than usual to make sure all was right with the nursery. Rose hadn't warmed to her either yet. Seemed she was all about Mia right now.

He dropped two ice cubes into a tumbler and poured himself a shot of vodka. Stepping outside, the cool salty air aroused his senses and he inhaled deeply. It was cleansing and peaceful out here.

To his left, movement caught his eye. He found Mia standing at the outer rim of the veranda where a low white stone wall bordered the sand. She watched the waves bound upon the shore. And Adam watched her. Breezes lifted the hem of her loose-fitting blouse, her long dark hair whipping at her back, her feet bare. She looked beautiful in the moonlight, and Adam debated going to her. He couldn't trust her. The lies she'd told him, the deceit she'd employed that had gotten them all to this point, painted an indelible mark on his soul. He'd be a fool to let her get under his skin again.

And Adam Chase was no fool.

Yet, he was drawn to her... Something was pulling at him, urging him to walk toward her and not stop. He had to see her. To talk to her. It was unlike anything he'd ever felt before. He took the steps necessary to reach her.

His footfalls on the stone alerted her to his presence. She turned to him. "Adam."

"Can't sleep?"

She shook her head. "I'm kind of keyed up. All these changes." Her shoulder lifted. "You know what I mean?"

"I think I do."

He shook his glass and the ice clinked. "Would you like a drink?"

Her eyes dipped to his glass. "No thanks. It's late. I should go check on Rose."

"I just did. I was in there before I came outside. She's sleeping."

Mia held a remote video receiver in her hand. She glanced at it and nodded. "I can see that."

"A pretty cool invention," he said.

"The best. I don't know how I'd ever get more than five feet away from her room without it. Even so, I get up during the night to check on her. It's a habit. Like I said, I really should go in."

"Am I disturbing you, Mia?"

Her gaze drifted to his mouth, then those amazing eyes connected to his. "It's your house, Adam," she said softly. "I might ask you the same thing. For all I know, you might have a nightly ritual of having a drink outside by yourself."

"Just me and my thoughts, huh?" If she only knew the pains he went through not to think. Not to let the demons inside. He sipped vodka and sighed. "You don't have to walk around on eggshells while you're here. For now, this is your home. Do whatever you please." Under a beam of moonlight her smooth olive complexion appeared a few shades lighter. He remembered touching her face, the softness under his fingertips when he'd kissed her. "We're going to be seeing each other a lot. I mean, my main focus is Rose. I want her to get used to me."

She turned away from him. "I get it. You're stuck with me. If you want to see Rose, I come along with the deal. Is that what you're trying to say?"

"It's just fact, Mia. And I can think of a lot of worse things than being stuck with a gorgeous woman living under my roof."

Mia snapped her head around, her eyes sharp and searching, her lips trembling.

Just days after meeting her, she'd gotten to him. She'd warped his defenses and he'd let her in a little. She'd made him think long range…he hadn't been that happy in a long time. But the path she'd led him down was broken and dangerous. He was too careful a man to venture in that direction again.

Boisterous voices carried on the breeze and reached his ears. Adam peered down the shoreline and made out half a dozen teens tripping over themselves, slinging loud drunken words, many of them profane.

He grabbed Mia's hand. "Shh. Come with me," he said leading her into the shadows behind a five-seat sofa. "Duck down."

He slouched, tugging her with him. They landed on their butts on the cold stone.

"What are you doing?"

"Shh," he repeated. "Lower your voice. It's the kids who've been vandalizing the beach," he whispered. "I still owe them for leaving that broken bottle in the sand and hurting you."

"How can you be sure they're the same kids?"

"Doesn't matter. News travels fast. They'll put the word out not to come here anymore."

"So, what's the plan?"

"Come with me and I'll show you."

Moving through the shadows, they entered the house. Adam left Mia at the foot of the stairs. "I'll check on the baby on my way back," he said.

Three minutes later, dressed in shorts and running shoes, he nodded at Mia as he reached the bottom step. "Not a peep out of her. She's still sleeping. Come—follow me outside."

They stayed out of the light as they returned to the spot near the sofa. "Okay, here's what I want you to do. Give me five minutes and be sure to watch. You'll get a kick out of it."

Adam explained the plan. Then he slunk through the darkness to the house next door that he'd once leased to his friend, country superstar Zane Williams. Zane was gone now, living back in Texas with his fiancée, and the house was empty. Well out of view, he trekked down to the shoreline and began jogging along the bank, heading toward the kids. He came upon them appearing as a midnight runner working up a sweat and breathing hard. Just as he reached them, he dug his heels in the sand and hunched over, hands on knees, and pretended to be out of breath. "Hey...guys." A dozen eyes watched him. "Anybody...have...some water?"

"Water?" one of the kids said. "Does it look like we have water?"

The kid tipped his bottle and slurped down beer. Then the big shot slung the bottle and it whizzed right by Adam's head. A crash competed with the roar of the waves as the bottle shattered against a metal ice bucket. Shards of glass scattered onto the sand. Adam ground his teeth. Maybe he should call the police.

Then one curly-haired boy stepped up and a plastic bottle of water was pushed into his hand. "Here you go, man. Drink up. You look like you could really use this."

The kid had compassion in his eyes. Okay. No cops. They were just stupid kids. They couldn't be more than sixteen years old. "Hey, thanks a lot. You know," he said, rising to his height and uncapping the bottle. "Just a heads-up, but you should be more careful. I mean, coming here and boozing it up right under the nose of a retired police captain."

"What?" the big shot said. "No way."

"Yeah, he moved into that house a few weeks ago." He pointed to the empty house. "I see his wife outside most nights watching the waves as I run by."

The boy craned his head in that direction. "That's far away. I can't see anything. Which means they can't see us."

"Okay, suit yourself. But I hear the captain's a hard-ass about underage drinking. Just a warning to you. Thanks for the water." Adam began jogging away. A siren bellowed, the sound screaming and urgent, disrupting the quiet of the night. Adam turned and looked into the big shot's eyes, wide now and panicked, his innocent years showing on his frightened face. The boys jumped to attention, all six of them darting fearful glances at each other.

One of them shouted, "Run!"

And they flew out of there, leaving their booze behind, kicking up sand and bumping into each other as they dashed down the beach. They'd run a good mile before they'd stop. The run and fright alone should sober them up.

Adam jogged over to Mia, who came out of hiding, holding the siren in her hand. She turned it off. "Did you see them run?" he asked.

"I sure did. Wow. This thing sounds like the real deal. Where did you get it?"

"It's a long story, but it's from my lifeguarding days. Sounds authentic because basically it is." Adam glanced down the beach, his mouth beginning to twitch. He hadn't had that much fun in a while. "I doubt they'll ever come back. Some might've learned a lesson. I can only hope."

He turned to find Mia smiling at him, her eyes warm and gentle. His heart began to thump, and blood pumped hard and fast through his veins.

One smile. One gentle look.

It shouldn't be that easy for Mia to affect him.

"You did this because they hurt me?"

"Yeah," he admitted. "They shouldn't be drinking at their age. Disturbing the peace and—"

Her lips touched his cheek in a kiss that was chaste and thankful. Her hair smelled of sweet berries.

"Mia," he said, folding her into his embrace.

"Adam, what are you doing?"

He whispered, "If you're going to thank me, do it right."

Mia came up for air a minute later. Her lips were gently bruised from Adam's kisses. The taste of him still lingered on her mouth. As he held her in his arms under the moonlight, she trembled.

It was crazy. This couldn't happen. They had a tentative relationship at best, and throwing romance into the mix would complicate everything. Adam clearly wasn't her biggest fan, and yet how could she forget how wonderful those first few days had been between them, when he didn't know who she was or what she'd done?

She hadn't forgotten about how his touch once made her giddy. How, before the truth was revealed, she had been lost in the moment and had almost given herself to him. Good thing that hadn't happened,

"Now, that was a proper thank-you." His hot breath hovered over her lips and she thought he would kiss her again. And once again, she might not stop him.

The baby's cries interrupted him. "Rose," she said, reaching for the baby monitor on the sofa and glancing at it. "She's awake, Adam. Fussing around."

Adam took the monitor from her hand and also looked.

"I've got to go to her," she said, walking quickly toward the doors.

"I'm coming."

Adam caught up to her and entwined their fingers. They headed upstairs together and when they reached the threshold to the nursery, Mia stopped and turned to him. "Maybe you should stay out here," she said.

Adam's head shook. "No, I'm coming in. She has to see me here. It's better that I'm with you."

"Okay." Rose's cries stopped the minute she saw Mia. She picked her up and cupped her head, kissing her rosy soft cheeks. "I know, my baby girl. This is all so new for you. But I'm here now. And so is your daddy."

Mia turned Rose toward Adam. She took one look at him and immediately swung her head in the opposite direction.

"Hi, Rose," he said anyway. "Sorry you can't sleep. Daddy can't, either."

Something lurched in Mia's heart as Adam spoke so tenderly and patiently to Rose. And hearing him call himself "Daddy" brought tears to her eyes. Her stomach ached. It seemed to do that a lot lately. Losing Rose would destroy her, she was sure, but how could she possibly not encourage the baby to know and love her father?

Mia turned so that Rose faced Adam. "Will you let Daddy hold you while I get you a bottle?"

Adam put out his arms to his daughter. Rose tightened her grip around Mia's neck, squirming up her body. Mia tried to pry her off, but Rose was determined not to go to her daddy. Mia didn't fight her. She stepped away from Adam and strode to the other side of the room. "It's okay, baby girl. It's okay. Adam, maybe you could warm up her bottle? I'll rock her."

Adam nodded and walked out of the room.

While he was gone, Mia changed the baby's diaper and then plunked down on the glider and began rocking the baby. By the time Adam returned, Rose was calmer and relaxed. Quietly, he handed Mia the bottle and sat cross-legged on the floor, facing them. Rose sucked on the bottle, keeping a vigilant eye on Adam. He said nothing, merely watched as Rose's eyes eventually closed. There were a few halfhearted attempts to suck the last inch of the formula down before Rose fell back to sleep.

"She's out," Mia whispered.

Adam nodded, the yearning in his expression touching something deep inside.

"Do you want to put her into the crib?" she asked.

"She'll wake if I do that." His voice was quietly bereft. Adam believed Rose had a sixth sense about him.

"No, I can almost guarantee you she won't wake up. She's out."

A childlike eagerness lit in his eyes and he stood. "Yes, then. Hand her to me."

Mia rose from the glider and transferred the baby carefully into Adam's arms. The baby didn't move a muscle. Mia sighed, grateful Rose didn't make a liar out of her.

Holding the infant in his arms, Adam's expression changed. The hard planes of his face softened. His gunmetal-gray eyes melted into longing, pride and love. It was beautiful to see.

But heartbreaking, too.

Mia stood back, away from Adam, overseeing him putting Rose down to sleep.

Not a whimper from Rose as her body touched down on the baby mattress.

Standing over the crib, Adam watched the baby sleep. Mia turned away, leaving the two of them alone. The bonding was happening right before her eyes. She was facilitating it to some degree. It was the right thing to do, but that didn't stop fearful jabs from poking her inside reminding her, her days with Rose at Moonlight Beach were numbered.

Saturday afternoon, Mia was just walking into the house with Rose after working a half a day at First Clips when she spotted Adam at the edge of the patio in very much the same place they'd kissed the other night. "Come on, Rose," she cooed. "Your daddy didn't see you this morning." Adam had made it clear he expected to see Rose at every opportunity. Mia couldn't balk at that. Or that Rose needed the fresh air. Most of her days were spent inside the salon.

She plopped a sunbonnet on Rose's head to shield her eyes from the sun. The hat matched a purple-and-white Swiss polka-dotted dress and bloomers that Adam had given her. She pictured him venturing out to shop for baby clothes and, well, she just couldn't grasp that notion. Yet Mary had insisted Adam had done the shopping with no help from her. She had to admit Rose looked especially adorable today.

With Rose in her arms, kicking her bootie-socked feet happily, Mia ventured outside. That beautiful kiss he'd planted on her hadn't been discussed or repeated. She'd thought that after she'd helped Adam chase off those teens, they'd broken new ground. Not the case apparently. Adam had retreated, probably kicking himself for letting down his guard and showing some emotion.

"Adam, we're home."

He turned around, but it wasn't Adam at all. The man had similar sharp features, a chiseled profile, strong jaw and shoulders just as broad. Stepping closer, she noted he wasn't nearly as tall and his eyes were a deep and mesmerizing blue. There was kindness on his face and a grin that touched something delicate in her heart as he gazed at the baby. "Sorry to disappoint. I'm Brandon. Adam's younger brother."

He put out his hand. "And you are?"

"Mia." She blinked. Adam hadn't told his brother about her and the baby?

They shook hands. "And who's this pretty little thing?"

She couldn't help responding kindly to him. He had a beautiful baritone voice that elevated as he asked about the baby. "This is Rose."

"Rose? Named after a flower," he said, his voice lowering, a veil dimming over his eyes. "Well nice to meet you two stunning ladies," he said. His eyes shined again. "I'm waiting for Adam. Mary said he's due back soon."

"He must be at the office. I think he had a meeting."

Brandon eyed her curiously, the smile never leaving his face. She didn't know what to say to him. Should she spill the beans? Adam was such a private person he might never forgive her if she did. It might be grounds for him tossing her out of the place.

"Is there something I should know? Am I an uncle?"

Mia shuddered.

Brandon's affable expression changed. "Sorry. She's got my brother's eyes."

There was no way around it. Brandon had guessed the truth. "Yes, Rose is Adam's child. I'm her aunt Mia."

"Aunt?"

She nodded. "It's a long story—better to be told by Adam, I think."

Brandon stared at her and then focused on his niece. "I'm an uncle."

Footsteps on stone had her turning to find Mary heading their way. *Thank goodness for the interruption.*

"Lunch is waiting, if you're hungry. I've got coffee, tea and lemonade ready in the kitchen."

Mia was famished. She'd eaten very little that morning. Rose had been in a mood and she'd missed breakfast. She should refuse, but how rude would it be to make Adam's brother eat alone? "Thanks, Mary."

"Shall I warm up a bottle for the little one?" Mary asked.

"I gave her a bottle a little while ago, but I appreciate the offer."

They entered the kitchen and ate lunch together, while the baby played quietly in the playpen. Brandon respected her wishes and didn't ask too many questions about the situation with Rose, other than how much she weighed at birth, how old she was and how Adam was taking to fatherhood. She skirted around the last question and turned the conversation to him. She found out he was a charter pilot working out of an Orange County airport and loved flying. He spent the remainder of their lunch speaking about his escapades in foreign countries, dealing with Homeland Security, and he told a few outrageous stories about the celebrities he'd flown around the world.

Rose began to cry and Mia rose immediately. As she lifted her out of the playpen, the baby whimpered still and Mia knew she had no time to lose. Rose could bellow with the best of them. "Sorry, she's hungry now. I've got to warm a bottle."

Brandon stood and walked over to her, holding out his arms. "No problem. Can I help?"

Mia tried not to let her eyeballs go wide. He didn't know

what he was asking. "Oh…uh. She's squeamish around strangers. I don't think she'll go to you."

"Can we try?" He had persuasive eyes, clear and so startling crystal blue a person could definitely lose their way in them.

"Sure." One second and he'd be handing her back.

"This is your uncle Brandon, Sweet Cheeks. He wants to hold you while I make your bottle."

Mia made the transition carefully, and Rose, the little sprite, didn't make a peep as Brandon settled her into his arms. He began moving, walking, pacing and rocking her as Mia looked on. Astonished, she'd almost forgotten about warming her bottle. "She's a sweet one," he said.

Mia gulped before giving him a smile. The baby was putty in his arms. Was that a good thing? Maybe Rose was finally coming around.

She made quick work of heating the formula in a bottle warmer. Once done, she placed the bottle above her arm and let a few drops drip onto her wrist. Brandon watched. "A test in case it's too hot."

"Gotcha." The baby was fascinated by him. She kept looking into his eyes, responding to his voice.

"I usually feed her in the living room. Mary likes that we're using that room."

Brandon followed her and sat down fairly close on the sofa. "Mind if I feed her?"

"Uh…no, I don't mind." The baby might even let him.

Mia handed him the bottle and the baby latched on to the nipple right away. She slurped and made sucking noises. "She's quite a guzzler." He chuckled and seemed comfortable holding an infant.

"She is growing like a weed."

Brandon took his eyes off the baby to give Mia a look. "I knew a Mia once, an older Italian woman who herded sheep. I can tell you stories…"

"Please do," she said. She enjoyed his company. He

was a charming, funny man who wasn't afraid to talk about himself, and she didn't mind the distraction from his brother, who would rather have a root canal than smile.

They were quietly laughing, Brandon just finishing a story about his crazy stay in Siena, the baby peacefully asleep in his arms, when Adam walked into the room. He stopped midway and gave Mia a cold glance before sending a grim look to his brother. His eyes were filled with indignation.

"Brandon." He kept his voice low, menacing. "What are you doing here? I didn't expect you until Monday."

"There was a change in plans."

Adam's mouth twisted in an unbecoming snarl. "There always is."

"Sorry, bro. I didn't think it would be a problem."

"It is a problem."

Adam frowned at Mia. There'd be no more smiles today for anyone.

"The baby is a stunner, Adam. Congratulations."

Adam blinked, his gaze shifting from her to the baby. "It's none of your concern, Brandon."

"Hey, you're a father, Adam. And that makes me this one's uncle. That's something to celebrate. Isn't she the reason you summoned me here?"

Adam's teeth clenched. He kept his focus on Rose now, in his brother's arms. Mia could only imagine what thoughts plagued his head. The baby wouldn't go to him, yet she took to Brandon, Adam's obviously estranged brother, like peanut butter to jelly.

"Does Mom know she's a grandmother?" Brandon asked.

Adam shook his head. "Not yet."

Mia rose from her seat. "Maybe I'd better let you two talk this out. Brandon, I'll take the baby—"

"Leave her be, Mia." Adam's voice was rough, his gaze

chillier than a deep freeze. "I don't want to break up your little party."

"It's not a party, for heaven's sake, Ad—"

He faced her, betrayal shining in his eyes. "Did you tell him everything?"

"She told me nothing," Brandon interjected in her defense, which only seemed to irritate Adam further.

"I'm asking Mia," he said, enunciating each word.

Defusing the situation was tricky. "No, I only told him that Rose was yours and that I'm her aunt. I thought it best for you to explain the details," she said.

He pinned her down. "That's all?"

She nodded and glanced at Brandon. "He was kind enough not to pressure me with questions."

"My brother's a regular Mr. Nice Guy."

Brandon rose now, careful with the baby in his arms. "Adam, don't take your sour mood out on Mia. Okay, so I showed up a few days early. My bad. Obviously, you've got issues going on here that you need to work out. I'll leave and come back another time."

Adam gave his head a shake. If he hoped to clear away his foul mood, it didn't work. "No. I need to talk to you. Tonight. We'll talk after dinner."

Brandon approached Adam with the baby, ready to hand her to him. Mia immediately stood and intervened. "I'll take her."

Wouldn't that just put a perfect ending on this afternoon for Rose to leave Brandon's arms only to start sobbing uncontrollably when Adam took hold of her. The scene played out in her head with HD clarity. She couldn't allow that to happen.

Brandon swiveled around, and opened his arms enough for Mia to gently take Rose from him. Little sleepyhead kept on sleeping, thankfully.

"Like I said, don't let me break up your little party. I have work to do."

Adam stalked out of the room leaving Brandon and Mia standing there, dumbfounded.

Seven

Adam pushed his hands through his hair half a dozen times as he paced the floor in his home office. He'd deliberately set his office in the front of the house, so he wouldn't be distracted by the roar of the ocean, beachgoers' voices carrying inside the room or a brilliant sun setting over the California shoreline. His windows open, sea breezes blew inside and ruffled the papers lying on his drafting table. He walked over and put a pewter paperweight over them. He wasn't going to get any work done today.

Brandon was here. It had been two years last Christmas since he'd seen him. His mother had insisted her boys share the holiday with her. They'd gone to her home at Sunny Hills and spent nine hours of rigid politeness being around each other. His mother's attempt at reconciliation hadn't worked and it had been awkward as hell. Adam wasn't ready to forgive Brandon for stealing Jacqueline away. Brandon, in one way or another, had been the source of pain for him all of his life. Yet, Brandon was the son whom his mother loved most. Deep down, Adam thought his mother had never forgiven him for what happened to Lily, though she'd never admitted that to him. Adam gnashed his teeth. Hell, he'd never forgiven himself. And he'd never divulged to his mother Brandon's part in Lily's death. Only Adam knew the absolute truth about what had happened that day.

Earlier today, when he'd seen Brandon holding Rose,

acid had spilled into his gut. He'd held back a barrage of curses. Brandon, the charmer, had already won Rose over, while Adam stood on the sidelines waiting and hoping his little baby would come to accept him.

Later that night over dinner, all was quiet. Mia didn't say a word that wasn't directed to the baby. Brandon was treading carefully, too. Several times, he'd caught Brandon shooting Mia conspiratorial sideway glances. Somehow Adam had become the villain.

Fine by him.

He was too wound up to give a damn.

Mia rose from the table after her meal and lifted the baby from her playpen. Rose clung to her neck so sweetly Adam ached inside. "I think we'll turn in early tonight," she said. "Good night, Brandon. Adam."

The sun had just set and it was especially early for her to hit the sack. Even little Rose didn't go to bed until nine. Mia wasn't fooling him. He'd behaved badly earlier this afternoon and she was annoyed with him. He probably deserved her scorn. And it was better that he speak with Brandon in private anyway. He was ready with a condensed version of the story to tell his brother about Rose. He didn't need Mia interjecting facts.

"Good night, Mia," Brandon said, rising to his feet. "Nice meeting you. And give that little one a good-night kiss from Uncle Brandon."

Mia smiled warmly at him. "I'll be sure to."

She was halfway out the door, when Adam spoke up. "I'll be up in a little while. Keep her awake until I get there."

Mia whirled on him instantly, shooting him twin green daggers with her eyes.

Great.

"Rose will sleep when she's tired, Adam, which I think was about five minutes ago. We're not waiting up."

He rolled his eyes. "Fine. Good night, then."

As soon as she left the room, Brandon grinned like a schoolboy. "You sure know how to charm them."

He bounded up, striding out of the kitchen to the bar outside on the patio. Fresh briny air smacked him in the face, and it was far gentler than Mia's reprimand. Technically, he could demand that she obey his wishes. He was Rose's father. He had all rights when it came to his daughter, but he'd never pull that card on Mia. Not unless she gave him good reason to.

He grabbed two highball glasses from underneath the white-and-black granite-topped bar and poured them both a drink. Brandon preferred bourbon, but Adam wasn't feeling especially generous tonight. He poured vodka into both glasses and handed him one as he walked up. "I'm going to make this quick. Want to take a seat?"

"Okay." The iron legs of the chaise scraped across the stone decking as Brandon pulled the chair out and sat down. He lifted his glass. "Thanks," he said and took a sip. His facial muscles tightened as he swallowed the strong liquor and leaned back.

Adam didn't want to start out on a bad note with his brother. He was ready to put the past behind him for his mother's sake, but having Brandon show up unannounced today and finding him holding his baby, his perfect little child who couldn't stand the sight of her own father, had snapped his patience.

He didn't like seeing Mia's eyes go warm and gooey over Brandon, either.

He dismissed that notion. Mia wasn't his concern. His mother and his child were his priorities now.

"So, tell me about the kid, Adam. She's yours—that much I know. And her mother is gone?"

He nodded. "Mia's sister died shortly after the birth."

"That's rough. Were you two close?"

"No, it wasn't like that. We barely knew each other."

"But you're certain the baby is yours?" Brandon asked.

"She is. DNA tests confirmed it. She's got the Chase birthmark, if DNA wasn't enough proof." A wry laugh erupted from his chest.

"No kidding. And what about Mia?"

"She spent months raising her and now she's moved in here, helping to make Rose's transition easier."

"Man, you sound like you're talking about some business merger or something. It's clear Mia loves that child. What about you?"

"Of course I love Rose. She's my daughter." It was love at first sight. On his part, anyway.

"You didn't pick her up when I tried to hand her to you. I haven't seen you hold her. And what's with you ordering Mia around like she's your indentured servant?"

Adam drew oxygen into his lungs. The chilly air helped keep his hot temper at bay. "None of that is important right now." He wasn't going to reveal how Mia had duped him when they first met. How she'd been doing her own form of investigation to make sure he was father material. Or that his daughter screamed blue murder when he tried to hold her. Wouldn't Mr. Charming have a good laugh over that one? "Look, I had an affair with Mia's sister. It wasn't serious and it ended mutually. I only learned weeks ago from Mia that Rose was conceived when we were together.

"So now I've got the baby here and we're trying to figure it out. Rose will always live with me."

"So you and Mia aren't…"

Adam shook his head a little too vehemently. "No. She's gone as soon as we feel Rose has acclimated to…the surroundings."

"Gone? Isn't that cold, Adam? She loves that child. It's clear Rose has formed a strong attachment to her. Who wouldn't? Mia's sweet and gorgeous and—"

"Brandon, lay off, okay? I said we're trying to figure it all out. And what makes you an expert on Mia D'Angelo anyway? You've known her for less than six hours."

"We talked. I have good instincts about people. She's a keeper."

Adam clenched his jaw. Was his brother really trying to give him romantic advice? "Do you want to know why I asked you to come here?"

"Has something to do with Mom. Her birthday's coming up." Brandon sipped his drink.

"That's right. It's her seventieth, and she wants only one thing from us."

"I can only guess."

"You got it. She wants us to patch up our differences. She wants to see her family whole again." It would never be, without Dad and Lily, but that was beside the point.

Brandon shoved the tumbler aside and leaned in from his nonchalant position on the chair. His elbows came to rest on the patio table. "I've tried, Adam. But you weren't ready to hear me."

Adam stared toward the ocean. The swells were high now, breaking on the shore in white foam that cleansed the sand. If only he could cleanse away the bitter pain that seeped into his soul that easily. Maybe that's what he was hoping for with those daily dawn swims, to wash away all the bad things in his life.

Brandon had always been at the very core of his pain. He'd been selfish and self-serving as a young boy, but Adam had never told his mother the true story. Because ultimately, he'd been the older one. He'd been responsible for Lily. "I'm listening now, Brandon."

"You're doing this for Mom."

He shrugged. "Does it matter why?"

Brandon drew a deep breath. "I guess not. I never meant to hurt you, Adam. As much as you may not want to hear this, I swear to you—Jacqueline and I never went behind your back."

Adam looked into his tumbler, sighed and then polished off the rest of it. He let the burn of alcohol settle in his gut before turning to face his brother. "No. You did it right in front of me."

"Not true. I admit, I fell for her from almost the moment I met her. Right here in this house. But she was your girlfriend, Adam. And I saw how much you cared for her. I never acted on my feelings. I never flirted. I never—"

"You were just your usual charming self."

"I am who I am."

Adam scoffed. "You're saying you couldn't help yourself?"

"No, that's not what I'm saying. You have to believe me. I fell hard for her, but never once thought about trying to come between you. I pretty much kept out of your hair. If you remember, I hardly showed up around here while you were dating. And when you two broke up, I struggled with that, but I didn't call her. I wanted to. I was in love with her, Adam. I'm sorry, but that's the truth. And I tried not to think about her. I figured out of sight, out of mind. Then one day, out of the blue, she called me. She had a friend who wanted to charter a flight for a special anniversary party. It began just by talking on the phone. A few dinners later, we were both in love. That's exactly how it happened, Adam. She didn't break up with you because of me."

Adam's mouth tightened. He gazed out to sea again, nodding his head. What was done was done. He'd have to live with Brandon's explanation for now. It had been six years. Jacqueline was out of the picture and his sister Lily wasn't ever coming back. If mending fences with Brandon would make his mother happy, he'd do it. "Okay. I understand."

Brandon slumped back against the chaise, his eyes incredulous. "You do? Just like that? For years, you've kept your distance. Now, you believe me?"

He'd recently discovered that he no longer cared about the situation with Brandon and Jacqueline. As far as he was concerned, it was ancient history. "I believe you didn't know how much it would affect me."

"We didn't sneak behind your back."

"Got it."

Though in Adam's rule book, he'd never go after his brother's girl, broken up or not. "Now, can we talk about Mom's birthday?"

"Sure…" Brandon smiled with a gleam in his eyes, reminding him of the young boy who'd always gotten away with stealing the last cupcake in the batch.

Adam tiptoed up the stairs after he and Brandon hashed out the details of their mother's birthday party. An hour had passed since Mia had taken the baby up to bed and he was certain the baby had already fallen asleep. Just watching Rose sleep was a relaxing balm, a way to calm his nerves and smooth out the kinks going on in his brain. She did that for him. He loved her with all of his heart, and it unnerved him how much she already meant to him.

He walked into the nursery lit by a Cinderella night-light and peered inside the crib, only to find it empty.

Slowly, he turned and crept out of the room. The door to Mia's room was ajar. He peeked inside and found the two of them asleep on the bed. Mia wore the same dress she'd had on during dinner, the hem of soft periwinkle cotton hiked up to her thighs. Her tanned legs were exposed and bent at the knees, protecting the baby with her body. She lay on her side facing him, two perfect breasts partially spilling out of her neckline and long raven strands of hair tickling her flesh as she took easy breaths. As sexy as she was in sleep, Adam only saw beauty now as she lay beside his child swathed with pink-and-brown teddy bears on her nightdress. Her breaths were strong and steady.

Tears stung his eyes, and the allure of their peaceful sleep brought him into the room. He stood over both of them for several seconds and recognized the yearning eating at him. He hadn't spent any time with Rose today. He'd missed his nightly ritual of holding her as she slept and laying her into the crib. It was such a small thing. One he never wanted to miss.

Nimbly, Adam kicked off his shoes and lay down on the bed. The mattress groaned and he winced, freezing in place. When no one stirred, he took great precautions stretching out his body, inching his way, trying not to wake either of them. Then he positioned his body exactly like Mia, a matching opposite bookend to complete the fortress around Rose's little sleeping self.

She was so small, so precious. Moving only the muscles necessary, he wound a curl of her blond hair around his finger. It was soft and as fine as silk. His eyes closed. He wanted to plant a loving kiss on her sweet cheeks. He wanted to speak to her, without her going ballistic on him, and tell her eye to eye how much he loved her.

When he opened his eyes, Mia was staring at him, those jade shards of ice from before melting to a bright warm glow. "Hi," she whispered over the baby. He could barely hear her.

"Hi."

"We tried to wait up."

So that's why they are on her bed tonight. After all her blistering, she thought enough to try to wait for him.

"Thanks. It took longer than I thought."

"You were grumpy tonight." She moved hair off her face, pushing the strands from her eyes. God, she was beautiful.

"My brother brings that out in me. He's gone. For now."

"Do you want to put her down in her crib?"

"Will that wake her?"

Mia glanced at the slumbering baby. "I doubt it. She's pretty tired."

He nodded. "Okay, then."

"You go on and do it. I'll stay here."

He stared at her for the beat of a second. "You're sure?" She wasn't going to oversee him putting the baby to sleep? He'd never done it without her watchful eye before.

"Yes."

Mia was a mystery to him. She'd lied to him, pretending to be an innocent bystander on the beach when they'd first met, and had kept up the deceit for days. Normally, Mia was extremely possessive about Rose. He didn't know what to make of her sudden generous attitude toward him. He certainly didn't trust her. Days earlier, he'd put the wheels in motion to find out what he could about her. More than she was willing to tell him. And he'd be interested in learning who Mia D'Angelo really was. Did she have any skeletons in her closet? He felt justified in his investigation because she had great influence over his daughter. A father had to protect his child, even from possible unknown threats.

Never taking his eyes off Rose, he slipped gently from the bed and bent to scoop her up. Fitting her little body across his arms, he braced her head with his right hand. She smelled of fresh diapers and baby shampoo, innocence and sweetness. He cradled her closer, absorbing all that goodness. She stirred from his movements, her hands fisting and her body arching in a stretch. He rocked her back and forth the way Mia had taught him, and she settled back into a peaceful sleep. Then he headed to the nursery and stood over the crib, hating to give her up. These were the only minutes in the day he could be this close to her. He could hold her all night and not tire of it, but he couldn't chance waking her. He laid her down, and she immediately turned her face toward the wall. She slept the same way he did. He smiled and after a few minutes inched away, his eyes on her as he backed out of the room.

Mission accomplished. He'd put his baby down all by himself. He felt over the moon.

Mia was waiting for him in the hallway. "Is she down?"

"Yeah, she stirred for a second but didn't wake up."

She smiled. "She does that."

Adam gazed into the warm glow of Mia's eyes again, the love shining through clearly despite the dim lighting. She looked mussed, a little tumbled and sexier than any woman he'd ever known.

"I'm glad you were able to put her down tonight."

"You waited up for me. Why?"

She shrugged. "You ordered it."

He took a step closer to her. Dangerous but he couldn't help himself. "If it came out that way, I apologize."

"I'm teasing, Adam. Do I look like a woman who'd cave to bullying tactics?"

"Definitely not." She looked like a woman who needed to be kissed and then some. "Why then?"

Her delicate shoulder lifted. "You were so tense around your brother, I figured you'd need Rose to soothe you."

"Oh, so *she* soothes *me*? Not the other way around. Is that what you're saying?"

"Uh-huh. Are you denying it?"

After a moment of thought, he replied, "No, I can't deny that."

"I didn't think so. Adam, what's up with you and your brother?"

He sighed and gave her a long look. He didn't want to have this conversation with her. He didn't want to have *any* conversation with her. "I don't want to talk about Brandon right now," he whispered, taking a step closer. "There are better things to do."

She gulped, and her gaze dipped to his mouth and lingered.

"Thank you for waiting up for me."

"It wasn't anything—"

"It was plenty," he whispered. His lips hovered over hers. Her breath smelled sweet and minty and when she sighed over his mouth, he could almost taste her.

"Adam," she whispered. A warning?

He thought she'd deny him a kiss, but instead she reached for his shirt collar and then slowly glided her fingers to the back of his neck. She locked her hands in place behind his head. The woman was unpredictable, and it only made her more appealing. Roping her around the waist, he pulled her closer.

She gazed at him, her eyes filled with the same warm glimmer she reserved for Rose. Resisting her now was impossible. He'd seen her laughing with Brandon, and that was all it had taken. If he had anything to say about it, Brandon wouldn't get within a mile of her.

He pressed his mouth to hers, and she fell into his kiss with a whimper of longing. A shudder ran through him. She affected him. And he couldn't help himself.

Her lips parted, and he didn't hesitate to plunge deeper and sink into the sweetness of her mouth.

He hadn't forgotten about that night in her apartment. He'd been lost in her and the heady way she'd responded to him. He'd touched the most intimate parts of her body, and she'd loved every second of it. During these past few nights, he'd lain awake in his bed thinking about her sleeping down the hall. Thinking about where that night would've led, if she hadn't dropped that bombshell on him.

There would be no bombshells tonight and he was ready to finish what he'd started.

Eight

"Adam, we can't." The words fell from her lips limply. They *were*, and she was helpless how to stop it.

His palm flattened against the center of her chest as he forced her back up against the wall. She was trapped by his body, cocooned in his heat. It was so unexpected, so thrilling a move her heartbeat began to pound up in her skull. His aggression excited her and his kisses wiped out any idea of a real protest. "Mia, tell me you don't want this and I'll back off."

He pulled away from her lips to trail hot moist kisses on her throat, gently nipping at her skin with his teeth. A path of fiery heat sprinted down her belly. She was dying with want, her traitorous body giving in to his passion, while a banner across her mind shouted no.

He whispered in her ear, "I'll take your silence as a yes."

A shiver ran through her, yet her mouth refused to open.

Adam kissed her then until she was breathless. His fingers fumbled with the spaghetti straps of her dress, sliding them down. Then with a few hastened tugs, the garment fell to a puddle on the floor around her feet.

She stood before him in her black bra and French-cut panties. He scanned over her body with a sharp intake of breath. "Mia," he said almost painfully. "What am I going to do with you?"

She had a pretty good idea and it didn't scare her. Well, just a little bit, considering who Adam was. He'd been her sister's lover once. She'd resigned herself to that already and didn't relate the mystery man she'd searched for with this living, breathing, sexy man who'd just picked her up into his arms.

He kissed her again and she held on to him as he carried her to his room.

She was lowered down on the bed, and he stood in front of her, flipping the buttons of his shirt. His chest appeared before her eyes, toned, rippled and solid. She sat there shaking, in awe of his upper body. If the lower half matched his brawn...

His eyes bored into her. "Come here, Mia."

The tone of his voice insisted on full obedience. Not that she would've disobeyed his command. She knew what she wanted and rose from the bed.

And then her world tipped upside down. Adam claimed her lips again and again and then he found other places to tease and torture with his mouth. His touch was magical, his hands knowing how to please, his fingers strumming her like a finely tuned instrument. Those firm demanding lips took her to heaven and back. He wreaked havoc on her body, one hand holding her in place while the other elicited moans of agonized pleasure.

"That's it, Mia. Fall apart in my arms."

His urgent command did the trick. The magician made her come apart at the seams, and she crumbled into a thousand wonderful satisfying pieces. She had the feeling Adam was just getting started.

He held her against him, cradling her so close she heard his rapid-fire heartbeat. Her hair was gently pushed off her face, tucked behind her ear and he placed easy quick kisses there to soothe her. She was loose like a rag doll and beautifully sated.

"Do what you want with me," he whispered.

Another thrill traveled south to regions of her body just satisfied. To have him at her mercy made liquid of her bones. Trembling, wicked thoughts entered her head. She was needy and throbbing again, and as she reached out to touch his slick moist skin, her hands shook. He was perfect, trim and muscled and as firm as granite. He shuddered under her hands, and she gazed into his eyes. They were soft, wistful, almost pleading. She had power over him. It was a heady notion and the biggest turn-on.

She lifted up to kiss him as she continued to probe his body. When her splayed hand reached beyond his belt buckle to tease the tip of his manhood, his breath came out as a sharp potent gasp. He was firm and large below the waist, another big-time turn-on.

"Touch me, sweetheart."

It was as much a dare as a request.

Mia wasn't one to back down from a dare. She covered the length of him with one hand and stroked over his trousers again and again. *Oh my.*

A deep barrel of a groan rose from his throat. And then she was being lifted again, Adam's soft curses ringing in her ears about enough foreplay or something. She hid a grin and was lowered rather unceremoniously onto a massive bed. "You said do what I want with you."

"And you're going to pay for that one."

"I'm waiting," she shot back. Where did she get her nerve?

He unbuckled his belt and removed his pants in a rush and joined her on the bed. *Oh my, again.* He had impressive architecture.

He rolled away from her and fiddled with a drawer in the end table. While he was doing that, she calmed herself by looking over the amazing bedroom. The corner room was angled and two entire walls were windows that looked out to sea. The rooms were tastefully decorated and—

He dumped five condom packets on the bed.

Her brows lifted. She had no idea Adam had such lofty plans for her. "Still waiting."

He groaned and grabbed her waist, lifting her above him. She settled, facing him in a straddle position over his thighs. "I want to see your face when I make love to you." Reaching up, he unhooked her bra and signaled for her to remove her panties.

No more fooling around. This was serious. *He* was serious, and the intensity in his eyes scared her a little. Her arms were braced by his hands and he began to massage them, up and down, caressing her limbs as if she were a precious jewel. It was pure heaven, and her anticipation grew. With a simultaneous tug of her arms, she fell forward, and he captured her mouth and kissed her soundly on the lips. The tips of her breasts touched his chest. The coarseness of his skin abraded her nipples, making them pebble up. He flicked his thumb over each one, and a shot of liquid heat poured down her body. She was beginning to ache in pleasant, searching ways. Adam kept it up, kissing her, touching her, making her come alive again.

She couldn't ignore his need, pressing firm against her belly. She touched him there and more soft curses rang from his lips. Hot silk in her hand, she pleasured him as he'd pleasured her, his moans and grunts encouraging her to go on.

Adam's eyes were wild now, smoky and dangerous. He hissed through his teeth, a warning for her to stop. Then his palms were on her waist, guiding her up onto him. They were both ready. She sank down into his heat and two instant moans of relief fell from their lips.

"So good," Adam muttered.

It was. She was filled with him, and it was only more beautiful when he began moving, his hands still on her waist, leading her, helping her find a rhythm that suited them both. He moved with her, slowly building up to a speed neither could maintain for too long. His hands went to her hips, and he rose up partway, encouraging her to wrap her legs around him. And it was like that for a while, each coming together, moving, looking into each other's eyes as he drove farther and farther.

He kissed her breasts, her throat, her chin, and when he reached her lips, he fell back against the pillows, taking her with him.

He arched his hips and pumped, keeping his eyes trained on her. Her hair spilled over the sides of his face and once again, he pushed the strands back, maintaining eye contact.

"Are you there?" he asked.

She nodded.

And then he unleashed the power of his body, sinking farther into her. She whimpered, her cries oddly quiet. It was so damn good, she was stunned almost silent.

Adam climbed with her, his body taxed but relentless. She let go a powerful release, and this time her mouth opened to a scream of pleasure.

Adam, too, made manly noises that seemed to promote his inner caveman. He huffed and grunted, and then she fell on top of him in a heap of boneless rapture.

By far, Adam Chase had given her the best night of loving in her life.

Mia rose from Adam's bed and tiptoed past the nightstand, where two remaining condom packets were left untouched. She was sore in places she hadn't been sore in years, but that wasn't the worst of it. She'd managed to have sex with Rose's father three times during the night. After the first time, the baby had woken and Mia went to her. Adam hadn't been far behind; he'd apparently become a light sleeper, since Rose had arrived here. Adam had warmed her bottle while Mia diapered her. Together, in the night-lighted room, they'd taken care of the baby. Once Rose had fallen back to sleep, Mia handed her off to Adam to put her down.

She'd been halfway to her own room when Adam took her hand and led her back to his big master bed. She hadn't gone kicking and screaming, and that was part of the problem. It had been so good between them she hadn't wanted the night to end. Adam hadn't let up on her and she'd met him touch for touch, kiss for kiss. After bout three, Adam held her tenderly in his arms, whispered soft words of her beauty, but he hadn't asked her to stay the night with him.

And once he'd fallen asleep, she'd returned to her own bed.

Now footsteps approached her room, and she listened carefully. Her door creaked open and Adam poked his head inside. They made eye contact and the door opened wider. Adam stood in the threshold, gazing at her in the predawn light. Disapproval marred his handsome features. "I'm going for a swim," he said. "Mary's not due for three more hours."

"Okay," she said. "I'll listen for Rose." If that's what he was getting at. She always listened for Rose, and this morning was no different.

He nodded, his gaze sharp on the covers she held up to her throat. After what they'd done to each other last night, it was a silly thing to do. But she felt vulnerable now and didn't know what he was thinking. Or feeling. Adam wasn't one to show emotion. Even now, after the passionate night they'd shared, his face was blank, his eyes unreadable, except for that note of disapproval she couldn't miss.

"Fine," he said. "You feeling all right?"

She'd had a hot night of sex with the handsomest man on the beach and all she could do was nod and answer, "Yes."

He blinked, stood there a few seconds and then closed the door.

Mia knocked her head against the pillows. What was that all about? Damn him. Why was he so closed off?

Was he not a morning person? How would she know— he never talked about himself. He didn't let anyone in. And what made her think he would ever let *her* in? Just because they'd satisfied their base needs last night didn't mean he would actually confide in her about anything.

She refused to think of last night as a mistake, but a little voice inside her head told her that very thing, over and over.

Where they went from here was anyone's guess.

Grabbing the baby monitor, she rose from bed and walked to the bathroom. She used a dimmer switch to adjust the lighting just so, and set the controls on the whirlpool tub. The jets turned on with a blast and bubbles rioted around the oval bathtub. She lit a few scented candles and soon vanilla and raspberry flavored the air, the flickering flames reflecting off the water. She was never one to pamper herself, but today luxury was called for. With luck, the baby would sleep another hour or two.

It would give her time to come to grips about her strong feelings for Adam Chase.

The genius recluse.

Adam stood at the edge of the veranda, his foot atop the stone border, gazing at Mia and the baby playing a game at the water's edge. The baby was smiling and every so often a breeze would carry Mia's animated voice to his ears as she played toe-tag with the incoming waves. He sipped coffee from a steaming mug. How had his life gotten so complicated?

He'd woken up early this morning to find Mia gone from his bed. He'd wanted her there last night. And this morning, he'd wanted to wake to the sweet scent of her luxurious body, to see her hair splayed across the pillow. He'd wanted to trail kisses across her soft shoulders and whisper good morning to her.

He'd worried that he'd been too rough with her, too forceful, too demanding of her body. When he found her gone from his bed, he'd worried that he'd hurt her. Thoughts of last night flashed before his eyes. There wasn't a doubt in his mind that he'd given her pleasure, but how much was too much? And had it been a stupid, mindless mistake, to take his daughter's aunt to bed? Carnal desire aside, he didn't want to ruin things between them. Mia would be in Rose's life forever.

"Here Adam—take this to Mia." Something was shoved into his free hand. He hadn't heard Mary come up behind him, and he looked down at the wicker basket he now held.

"What is it?"

"Mia's breakfast. Yogurt and granola, toast and juice. She has the day off, but she didn't eat anything this morning. There's some other things in there, too, if you'd like."

He gazed at Mia again. She'd taken a seat on a blanket under one of his multicolored umbrellas, the baby propped in her arms. "No, I'm good right now."

Mary relieved him of his coffee mug. "Go on now. Take her the basket. I know you want to."

Mary's eyes twinkled. He nodded. "Fine, if you want to shirk your duties."

"That's me—always finding my way out of doing work around here."

Mary was the best housekeeper he'd ever had. She'd been with him since before he'd come to Moonlight Beach. He wouldn't want anyone else taking care of his home.

"Fine. Shirker."

"I'll be eating bonbons on the sofa in you need me," Mary said as she walked away.

"Smart aleck," he muttered and stepped onto the beach barefoot.

It was a short walk to where Mia had planted herself. He supposed she'd want to have *the talk*. Adam hated those "what happens now" questions that he couldn't answer. Since Jacqueline, the women he'd been with had been few and far between, but almost all of them wanted to know where they'd stood with him after a night of sex.

Once he reached the blanket, he crouched down, setting the basket next to Mia. "Here you go. Compliments of Mary. Breakfast."

Mia turned to him, her sunglasses shielding her eyes. She removed them and glanced at the basket. "That's very nice of her," she said and finally looked at him. Her eyes were a gorgeous shade of rich green, reminding him of morning grass on the pastures in Oklahoma. He was struck silent for a second. "I'll thank her when I go in," she said.

The baby stared at him, her lower lip jutting out and trembling. Her pout broke his heart all over again. What would it take for Rose to accept him?

"Mind if I join you?" he asked.

She hesitated for longer than he would've liked. "No, be my guest."

He scooted onto the blanket on the other side of the baby. He hated that he had to keep his distance from her to keep her happy. Maybe he should keep his distance from Mia, too.

Too late for that.

"You weren't hungry this morning?" He looked into the basket and found a dish of vanilla yogurt topped with granola and raisins, pastries, a bottle of orange juice and fruit.

"Not really. I had coffee."

"Yeah, me, too."

He watched the waves bound in and out. Her silence unnerved him. Had he done something wrong? Other than the obvious, making love to a woman he had no right making love to.

Her hair was pulled into a ponytail that extended to the middle of her back. She wore black shorts and a pretty white scoop-neck tank with a glittery pink tiara painted over her chest. Mia looked delicious in anything she wore.

"You didn't stay the night with me," he said finally. It had been on his mind all morning. "Why?"

He braced himself for her answer. While he knew darn well they shouldn't be entering into an affair, hearing her put a halt to it wouldn't be welcome news. He couldn't imagine not touching her again. She was under his roof and so darn beautiful; it would be the greatest test to his willpower to keep away from her.

"You didn't ask me to."

His mouth nearly dropped open. "I figured you'd know that I'd want to wake up with you."

"Adam," she said, sighing. "Are we really going to have this talk?"

This talk? *The talk?* "Well, hell yeah, we should talk. Don't you think so?"

"I don't see the point."

He clenched his teeth. "You don't see the point?"

"It's weird, Adam. That's all. You and me, after what happened between you and my sister. Are you making comparisons? Did I measure up?"

He blinked, obviously surprised. "Mia, what's going on between you and me has nothing to do with that. Well, indirectly it does, since if Rose wasn't born, I wouldn't have gotten to know you. What's done is done, Mia. I can't change the past. Is that why you're upset?"

"No, Adam. That's not it."

"Then what is it?"

Their voices were raised, and Rose's lips began to quiver. Her face flushed red, a precursor to crying that he'd come to recognize. Mia scrambled to her feet, taking the baby with her. "It's nothing," she said, her voice lower and steady for the baby's sake. "Nothing whatsoever. I'm going inside. The sun's getting too hot for the baby."

A few scattered rays of sunlight beamed through the clouds, hardly enough heat to warrant taking the baby inside. He rose to his feet. "Wait a minute, Mia. Don't leave. We need to figure this out."

"Is that an order?"

He sighed. He hated that she played the martyr. If she was confused, well, so was he. But what they shared last night, all night, was pretty damn amazing. "It's a request. What's gotten into you today?"

"You, Adam. You've gotten into me. How does it feel not having your questions answered? Not knowing where you stand? Not good? Well, welcome to my world."

Crap. He stood there mystified, watching her walk away.

What on earth did she want from him?

And when he figured it out, would he be able to give it to her?

"I can't believe my son didn't tell me about this little one, the minute he learned he was a father," Alena Chase said to Mia.

Mia sat next to Adam's mother on the sofa, with Rose seated comfortably on her lap. Alena's birthday celebration was set for six o'clock that night, and Adam had picked up his mother early to give her the news. He was off somewhere now, speaking to Mary and the catering staff.

Alena had a pleasant voice that hinted at her southern beginnings. Her eyes were a brilliant blue-gray very similar to Adam's, and she wore her thick white hair curled just under her chin in a youthful style. Her face was smooth for a woman her age and only crinkled when she smiled. There were plenty of smiles. She absolutely glowed around Rose. Mia could relate. She'd thought she might feel threatened by yet another Chase laying claim to Rose, but she didn't feel that way about Alena.

"I think it's taken Adam a while to come to grips with it himself," Mia said. She didn't come to his defense for any reason other than to keep Alena's feelings from being hurt. Leave it to Adam to let two weeks go by before he told his mother the truth. "I think he wanted to surprise you for your birthday."

Alena took Rose's small hand in hers and gave it a little shake and then stroked the baby's soft skin over and over.

"Such a sweet surprise. I can't even fault Adam—I'm too happy about becoming an instant grandmother today. It's the best gift in the world. Now I have my entire family here for my birthday."

Brandon sat down and scooted close to Mia, his arm resting behind her on the back of the sofa cushions. "That's just what you wanted, right, Mom?"

She nodded, her gaze never leaving Rose. "Yes. Just what I wanted."

Alena hadn't judged her. She hadn't asked a lot of questions, either. She wondered how much of the true story she'd gotten from Adam when he'd picked her up this morning. Adam, the great communicator.

Mia had made a special point to keep her distance from him all week. She couldn't out and out ignore him, because he expected to see the baby, but she'd found excuses to work later than usual at First Clips every day. There were a dozen good reasons why she needed to avoid him, but the main one popped into her head day and night and wouldn't leave her alone.

She was falling for him.

And that was a disaster in the making.

Adam walked into the room and all eyes turned to him. He took in their cozy scene on the sofa, his gaze lifting to Brandon's arm nearly around her shoulders. His nostrils flared a bit, and a tic worked his jaw. Surely, he didn't think that she and Brandon...

He took a seat opposite them, his back to the ocean, and spoke to his mother. "All is set for the party tonight."

"That's fine, son. I can't wait to introduce this little one to my friends."

Adam nodded. "She'll steal everyone's heart."

"She looks so much like Lily did at this age," his mother said, her eyes misting up.

Adam stared straight ahead, not saying a word. His throat moved in a giant swallow. On a Richter scale of curiosity, Mia registered the highest magnitude. Adam's life was one big mystery to her.

"Sorry Adam, I know you don't like to talk about Lily, but it's just that I feel she's—"

"Mom, she looks more like Adam, I think." Brandon intervened, giving each of them a glance.

"Actually, the baby has her mother's nose and mouth," Mia said softly, gazing at the baby in her arms. Her heart lurched. "She looks a lot like Anna."

Alena blinked, and then lowered her head. "Oh, dear. I'm sorry if I'm being callous." She seemed genuinely contrite. "I'm sure Rose has many of your sister's features. That poor girl, losing her life that way. You must miss her terribly."

"I do. Every day. We were close."

"I'm so smitten with the baby, I can hardly think straight. Can you forgive me?"

Mia nodded. "Yes. Of course. I understand."

Mary walked into the room to announce that lunch was being served on the veranda outside. It was her cue to escape the tension surrounding Adam's family. There seemed to be many unspoken words between them. "Rose needs a diaper change and a nap before the party. I'll take her upstairs now."

"I'll bring up your lunch if you'd like," Mary said.

"Oh, that's not necessary. I'm not very hungry. I'll come down later and eat something."

Mary tilted her head, a note of disapproval in her expression.

"I promise," Mia said. "I'll eat something in a little while."

Mary let it go with a nod. It was sweet the way Mary mothered her.

She made her escape to their rooms upstairs. It would be a big day for Rose, and she really did need a nap. She took one look at the baby making clicking noises and searching with her mouth for the bottle Mia had forgotten to bring up. "Oh, baby. What a dummy your auntie is."

"Is this what you're looking for?" Mia jumped and turned to Adam. He gestured, holding Rose's bottle. "It's ready to go. And, no, you're not a dummy. Maybe you're a little too anxious to get away from my family, though."

Mia's shoulders slumped. "Was I that obvious?" Adam looked a little worn around the edges. His face sported stubble, his eyes appeared sleep weary and not every hair on his head was in place. He looked approachable, normal, but still hot enough to heat her blood.

"Only to me."

"It's not your family, Adam. It's me. I feel…out of place. I know nothing about them, and I have no idea what you've told them about me."

"They know only what they need to know about you. All good things."

"You didn't tell them the entire truth?"

He cracked a rare smile. "Mia, really? You think I'd want them to know how I really came to meet you? What purpose would it serve?"

He was right and it eased her mind that he'd protected her from his family's mistrust and scrutiny.

"So they know nothing about how I—"

"No. They know you had trouble finding out who I was and that once you found me, you immediately told me I had a daughter. That's all they need to know."

"Okay, but I did what I did only because—"

"I know your reasons, Mia. No need to rehash them."

Adam set the bottle down beside the diaper changer and glanced at Rose. Mia had her diaper off and was cleansing her bottom. Adam reached for a diaper and opened it, his eyes, as tired as they appeared before, now beamed with love for his daughter. It transformed his whole face, and Mia would never tire of seeing that adoring expression on Adam. She lifted the baby's legs up a few inches, and Adam slid the diaper underneath her soft-cheeked bottom.

"We're becoming a well-oiled team," Adam said. "I'd like to think so anyway."

Mia finished diapering her and sat down on the glider. The baby latched on to the bottle instantly, guzzling the nipple and taking long pulls of formula.

Adam sat down on the floor beside the glider, watching her feed the baby. It was becoming a ritual, Adam waiting for the time when the baby slept, so he could hold her for precious moments and put her down into her crib.

Only minutes later, the bottle was sucked dry and the baby's eyes had drifted closed. When Mia nodded to Adam, he helped her up and the hand he'd placed on her shoulder sparked a riot of emotion. He hadn't touched her for days and she'd hoped to be immune, but that night of shared passion was never far from her mind. She'd done a good job of keeping her distance from him since, yet her body responded to him like no other man she'd ever met before. Drawing in her lips, she nibbled on them and sighed.

"Here you go." Carefully, she handed Rose off to him and walked out of the room. It was his special time with his daughter and Mia could grant him that. At any other part of the day, Rose didn't want to have anything to do with her father.

Mia was standing at the window in her room watching the tide roll in, when she heard a knock on her door. She turned to find Adam there. "Do you have a minute?"

"Is Rose down?" she asked.

"Sleeping like an angel."

"Shouldn't you be having lunch with your family?"

"I'll go down in a few minutes. My mother never tires of being with Brandon."

There it was again, spoken with no sarcasm, yet Adam's choice of words was very revealing.

"Come in."

He approached her and for a few seconds was quiet, standing by her side watching the surf curl into waves that beat upon the shore.

"What is it, Adam?"

He sighed and his gaze flowed over her. "It's you, Mia. You're doing your best to avoid me."

"I won't deny that."

His brows lifted as if he didn't expect her to be so blunt. "Why?"

Did he really want to have this conversation now, on the day of his mother's party? "Let's just say I don't find you…" She stopped. Was she really going to say she didn't find him appealing, attractive—she wasn't into him? Yeah, right. And the sun didn't rise in the east every day. "You and I aren't compatible." She shrugged. That would have to do.

"Liar."

"What?"

"We're very compatible. In case you're forgetting that pretty fantastic night together. I'm having a hard time forgetting it. And I heard no complaints from you that night."

She blushed. "I mean outside of the bedroom."

"How so?"

"Adam, you're a recluse. Not only do you hide inside your house—you don't engage with people. You're closed off. You give nothing of yourself away, and I already have trust issues with men. So, you see, it's impossible. Besides, there's Rose to think about."

"Leave Rose out of this. What do you mean, you have trust issues?"

"Something's clearly eating at you, and you won't tell me what it is."

"I don't know what you're talking about," he said, eyes wide as a schoolboy's.

"Okay, fine, Adam. If that's how you want to play this. There's really nothing much more to talk about. Now, if you don't mind, I have some work to do before the party tonight."

"Mia, don't dismiss me."

She lifted her face to his, shaking her head and wishing for things to be different. "Then tell me the truth, Adam." The plea in her voice was softly spoken. "Talk to me."

"I'll tell you one truth." He cupped her face in his hands and, before she knew what was happening, placed a solid, smoldering kiss on her lips. A guttural moan rose from her throat as he drew her closer, his body pressed to hers, hips colliding, chests crushing.

He ended the kiss abruptly and spoke over her bruised lips. "Compatible."

He was almost to her door, when he turned to her and tossed out, "For your own sake, stay away from my brother, Mia. He's trouble."

Nine

Trouble was charming. *Trouble* offered her a drink and bantered with her during the party, while Adam stayed back overseeing the celebration with his foot braced against the wall on the veranda. *Trouble* wasn't trouble at all. He seemed like a man eager to get to know his niece. Brandon would leave Mia and Rose's side and venture to the opposite end of the patio to entertain one of his mother's guests and then come back to say something clever to Rose. Mia had no interest in Brandon, other than he was Rose's uncle and so far, proved to be a pretty nice guy, yet Adam hadn't balked at the chance to warn her about him. Why?

"I can't believe she's my granddaughter," Alena said, rocking the baby gently, with the expertise only a mother would know. Rose seemed to enjoy it. So far, not a peep out of her as Alena held her. Adam had given Rose the outfit she wore today. It was a lavender satin little thing, with frills and lace, made by a designer. Her shoes and socks and bonnet all matched. Several of Alena's friends surrounded her, their gazes focused lovingly on grandmother and baby. Alena was in birthday heaven.

"She's lucky to have you," Mia said. She couldn't begrudge the baby the love of her grandmother. Rose deserved to be loved by everyone in her family.

Alena's eyes welled with tears. "Thank you. It's nice of you to say. I hope to be seeing a lot of her. She's the blessing I've been praying for."

"I think Rose would enjoy spending time with you, Alena."

Rose, as if on cue, began to fuss.

"There, there," Alena said, changing her position and rocking her a little more forcefully. Rose was having none of it. Her mouth opened to tiny cries that grew increasing louder. "Whoops, I think she needs her auntie Mia."

Alena transferred the baby into Mia's arms, just as a hush came over the twenty-five other partygoers. Mia turned to see what the big deal was all about. In walked Dylan McKay, only the most celebrated movie star of this decade, with a young woman on his arm. He smiled amiably at everyone and strode directly over to Alena. He took her hands in his. "Alena, happy birthday," he said, giving her a big smooch on the cheek.

Women had swooned over far less attention from Dylan McKay.

"Dylan, I'm very glad you came."

"I wouldn't miss it." Alena's face was in full bloom.

"This is Brooke, my little sis."

"Hi," Brooke said. She was very attractive and up until that moment, Mia suspected she knew what had been on everyone's mind when Dylan had walked in with her. Dylan McKay was fodder for the tabloids and the entire world supposedly knew who he was dating, made-up scandals or not. "Nice to meet you."

"The very same here, my dear. Thank you both for coming."

"I hear there's someone else for me to meet." Dylan turned her way. "Hi again, Mia," he said. "We've met once before." His daunting blue eyes bored into her, and she almost swooned herself.

"Yes, we have. Hello, Dylan. It's nice to meet you, Brooke."

Alena sent an adoring look at Rose. "And this gorgeous little babe is my granddaughter, Rose."

Mia wasn't new to celebrities. First Clips catered to a

high-end clientele, but she'd never spent time with anyone in the same caliber as Dylan McKay. Adam never mentioned to her he'd invited them, but of course, why would he break the mold? After that kiss today, her relationship with him was even more complex than ever.

Adam finally left his wall space and approached the group. "Dylan, Brooke," he said amiably. "Welcome."

Dylan nodded, his focus solely on Rose. "She's beautiful, Adam. Congratulations."

He extended his hand, and the two men shook. "Thanks. Can I get you and Brooke a drink?"

"Sure, I'll go with you. Brooke, are you okay here?" Dylan asked.

"Of course. You know I love babies. Do you mind if I hang out with you?" she asked Mia.

"Not at all," Mia said. "I'd like that."

"Great," Dylan said. "I'll be back in a little while."

Dylan walked off with Adam and Brooke turned her attention to Rose. "May I hold her?"

Mia smiled warmly. "You can try."

"So you're a daddy now?" Dylan said, taking a sip of Grey Goose. They stood a few feet from the bar, out of the way of the bartender, who was making cocktails for the guests.

Dylan's appearance impressed his mother's friends, but that was not why he'd been invited. Dylan truly cared for Alena Chase. She reminded him of his own mother, who was living a quiet life in Ohio as a retired school principal. And in his own way, Dylan McKay was old-fashioned about family. He was a good son and brother from what Adam could tell.

"It appears that way. It came as a shock, but I'm getting used to the idea."

Dylan glanced into the crowd surrounding Mia and the baby. "The baby also came with a pretty hot-looking nanny.

Or haven't you noticed?" He grinned that winning mega-watt grin that earned him millions.

"I've noticed. But don't let your imagination run wild. Mia isn't her nanny. She's Rose's aunt and she's off-limits." To every man here under the age of sixty, he wanted to add, which meant Dylan and Brandon.

"Possessive," Dylan said.

Adam shrugged. It did no good explaining the situation to Dylan. The guy formed his own impressions and usually they were dead-on. "Not really. Just looking out for my daughter's welfare."

"Hmm. Yeah, I can see that. She's living with you, isn't she?"

"Rose? Yes, she's my daughter."

"I meant Aunt Mia."

Of course that's what he meant. "It's a temporary arrangement. Now change the subject, Dylan."

"Okay, but first let me say I'm very happy for you. It may not be a perfect situation, but that baby will bring you a world of joy."

Dylan wanted to find a woman he could settle down and raise a family with. He'd dated a bunch of women already and hadn't found *the one*. The man loved kids and wanted a few of his own. Sometimes, fame came with a huge price, and he was never sure who he could trust, who was the real deal.

Adam could relate. He didn't trust easily anymore. He thought he knew what love was, but apparently he'd been wrong. Having his heart carved up and laid out on a silver platter could do that to a man.

"Your mom looks happy, Adam."

"She's getting exactly what she wants. Brandon and I have patched up our differences. The baby is the icing on the cake for my mother. A baby bonus."

"Yeah, well, babies have a way of softening people. So, you've forgiven Brandon?"

One night over a bottle of fifty-year-old Chivas Regal whiskey, Adam had divulged his heartache about Jacqueline and his brother to Dylan. He was the only person who remotely knew the story. Apparently, Dylan had been dumped once, too, before he'd become famous, and the scars had left an indelible mark on him.

"For the most part, yeah."

He glanced over to the fire pit. Brandon was standing beside Mia, and their laughter drifted to his ears. What did the two of them always seem to find so funny? Adam fisted his free hand as he sipped his drink.

Dylan followed the direction of his gaze "You sure? Because you're looking a lot like the jealous husband right out of my last movie about now."

Adam glared at Dylan.

"Hey, don't kill the messenger. Listen, if you're interested in her, you should do something about it. She's the whole package."

"How on earth do you know that?"

"Hell, Adam. I read people. And if she wasn't, you wouldn't trust your baby with her or look like you want to strangle your brother right about now."

Adam drew a sharp breath. "Shut up."

"You know I'm right."

"What happened to changing the subject?"

"Okay, fine. Are you going to Zane's wedding next week?"

Country superstar Zane Williams had been his other next-door neighbor on Moonlight Beach until he'd fallen in love with Jessica Holcomb, his late wife's sister, and moved back to Texas. "I am. How about you?"

"I'm bummed that I can't. I'm set to film up north next week."

"Are you taking Brooke with you?"

Dylan's gaze reverted to his foster sister, who was playing with little Rose. "No, Brooke's too busy with her new business. She's moving into her own apartment this week," he said. "Things are going well for her."

The chef interrupted his next thought. "Dinner is ready, Mr. Chase. Would you like to announce it, or shall I?"

"You do it, Pierre, and thank you."

Adam and Dylan walked over to the fire pit where Rose was staring at the stone gems casting off light and heat. She seemed fascinated by the crystallized display, and Adam got a kick out of seeing life through her untarnished eyes.

"Mom, we're ready for dinner. Chef made all of your favorites."

His mother looked up. "Mia and Rose will sit with us at our table?"

"Yes."

"And Brandon, too?" she asked.

"Of course, Mom. Today is all about family."

Mia's head lifted. Her eyes softened as they met his, and Adam winked at her.

She tilted her head to one side.

Then she smiled, a beautiful, heart-pulling smile that settled around his heart.

"The party was really nice," Mia said to Sherry on Monday morning as they prepared to open the doors at First Clips. The first appointments were due at nine. Sherry arranged her hairbrushes, combs and scissors, while Mia looked over the appointment book. Rose was perfectly happy swatting at the toys hanging over the handle of her infant seat. "Adam's mother is smitten with Rose. She said it was the best birthday of her life."

"I would imagine. Learning that she had an adorable granddaughter could only put a smile on her face. But, Mia, was it hard seeing her with the baby?"

Mia thought about it a second. "Not really. I thought it would be. Gram is the only grandmother Rose has known, so I worried that it might seem strange and, I don't know, kind of disloyal. But it wasn't that way at all. Alena is a warm person and she's careful not to be heavy-handed when it comes to Rose. She stayed over the weekend, and we got to know each other a little. For her birthday, I had a picture of Rose taken shortly after her birth blown up and framed. Alena cried when I gave it to her and told me how much she appreciated it. She left this morning and you should've seen her when she kissed Rose goodbye. It was really touching. "

"So, now it's just you and the hunky architect living in that big old mansion again?"

"Technically yes. But it isn't like that, Sherry."

"Okay, if you say so. Did I tell you how jealous I am that you partied with Dylan McKay? Mia, you're mingling with Hollywood royalty."

"About ten times this morning."

"Oh man, Mia. If I didn't love you so much, I'd hate you."

"Thanks… I think."

Rena walked in wearing a cerulean satin princess gown à la Cinderella. Her hair was piled up on her head; a tiara dotted with gemstones caught the overhead lighting. "Morning ladies. How's everyone today?"

"Dylan McKay was at the party over the weekend," Sherry announced.

"No way he was," Rena said. Contrary to her words, her face lit up. "He wasn't there, was he?"

"If I promise to tell you, you have to promise not to hate me."

Rena gave Sherry a glance. She was feigning a frown and nodding her head. Rena's eyes widened. "I promise," she said. "Now tell me all about it."

She recounted the brief conversations she'd had with Dylan to her friends, and as they worked through the morning, they managed to keep all their appointments on schedule. Five boys and seven girls were clipped and groomed and had walked out with smiles on their faces. By eleven-thirty, Mia's stomach growled. She hadn't eaten much that morning. As she headed to the back lounge, taking the diaper bag with her, she spotted Rena and Sherry ogling a man through the shop window.

"He's heading this way," Rena said. "Would you look at him? He's a ten, if I ever saw one."

"Ten and a half," Sherry added. "Bone structure counts extra, you know."

"I take it you're not talking about shoe sizes," Mia said, preoccupied with getting Rose's bottle out of the diaper bag.

"No, but oh man, Mia. This guy is hot. I bet he'd put your Adam to shame."

"He's not *my* Adam." She was curious enough to move over to the window beside her friends. She followed their line of vision and oh! Thump. The overfilled diaper bag slipped from her hand. She gulped. "That *is* Adam."

The girls shrieked. "That's Adam," Sherry said. "Oh, Mia. Now I really do hate you."

"Me, too," Rena said.

"Oh, be quiet, you two." What was he doing here? Adam was too busy perusing the storefront sign to notice the three of them all lined up, gawking at him.

The next thing she knew, he was reaching for the door-knob. The overhead chime rang out a rendition of the *Star Wars* theme and he walked in. The girls bumped shoulders, waiting in attendance. They probably looked like the Three Stooges on a bad day.

"Hello," he said, eyeing the girls first. Mia had to admit, their starship captain and princess getups were a bit distracting.

"Hi," the two chorused in unison.

Mia stepped up. "Adam, what are you doing here?"

He shrugged. After he lifted his shoulders, the beige

zillion-dollar suit he wore slipped right back into place. "I came to see your shop."

Rena made an obvious throat-clearing sound, and Mia got the hint.

"Oh, right. Adam, let me introduce you my friends. They staff the shop along with me. This is Rena and Sherry. Adam Chase."

He took both of their hands and gave a gentle one-pump handshake. "Nice to meet you ladies. I've heard good things from Mia about you."

"Same here," Sherry said. "I mean, Mia talks about you all the time."

Mia nibbled her lip.

Adam glanced at her, and she looked away.

"Where's Rose?"

"She's in the lounge, napping," Rena volunteered. "We take turns with that precious bundle. Sherry and I are her honorary aunties."

Adam nodded. "I know she's in good hands." He turned to Mia. "If you have a minute, I'd like to speak with you."

"Now? Here?" She was curious. Why couldn't it wait until she got home?

"Yes, if you have the time."

"Oh, um. Sure. Follow me and I'll give you the nickel tour. We can talk in the back room, and you can see Rose."

"Sounds like a plan."

It really did only take two minutes to show Adam the entire shop. They wound up in the lounge area where Rose was sleeping. "She's still asleep," she whispered. "Sometimes she sleeps in the infant seat and sometimes I put her down in the playpen. I keep this place spotless and she's in good hands with Rena and Sherry, so you don't—"

Two of his fingertips brushed over her mouth, stopping her from saying more. The pads were rough over her lips, but a sweet tingle washed through her anyway. "Mia, you don't have to explain. I'm not here to inspect the place."

"Then why are you here?"

"I came by to see where my daughter spends a lot of her time. And I came to ask you to lunch."

"Lunch? You want to have lunch with me?"

"You look surprised. Don't you take a lunch break?"

"Yes, but...why?"

He released a big sigh. "I'm trying, Mia."

"Trying to do what?"

"Not be so closed off."

They sat across from each other in a hole-in-the-wall restaurant in Santa Monica, three blocks away from her shop. Seaboard Café boasted the best seafood in town. The baby enjoyed the short walk in the stroller and was now sitting in her infant seat next to Mia, taking in the surroundings with inquisitive eyes. Mia's heart seemed to be in a perpetual state of melt mode lately. She'd gone gooey soft inside when Adam confessed he was trying not to be so closed off. For her? If only she could be sure. But oh wow, that seemed to come out of the blue. And it made her giddy.

Adam stood for a moment and removed his jacket. "You mind?"

She shook her head. He could undress in front of her anytime he wanted.

He unfastened his tie and folded it into his jacket pocket and then unbuttoned the first two buttons on a crisp cocoa-brown shirt. He'd come into the shop looking sharp and handsome, but he was no less gorgeous now. The girls would never let up on her now that they'd laid eyes on him.

He sat down, shot his daughter an adoring look and said, "I like your shop. It was hard to picture in my mind. Now, I can visualize children sitting in those chairs getting their hair cut."

"We still have our challenges. Sometimes we get a child who is frightened or stubborn. All the bells and whistles in the world won't get them to sit in the chair. Sherry has actually cut a child's hair, sitting in the rocket ship, while the child stood up. The kid absolutely refused to do it any other way. We have learned to be flexible."

"It's a great idea, though. A very unique approach for a hair salon. Was it your idea?"

"No, I'm not that imaginative. It was Anna's. She was the mastermind of First Clips."

Adam nodded. And then hesitated. His lips pursed, tightening up. He seemed to have something to say, but he kept silent.

"What is it?" she asked.

"Your sister. I'm sorry she died, Mia."

Mia's heart pounded hard, the way it did whenever Anna's death was brought up. "Thank you."

"What you said about me comparing you to her, that isn't true. It never crossed my mind."

Mia's eyes narrowed on him. "Not even a little?"

"No. Not even a little."

"I wasn't too happy with you when I said those things."

"I know."

The waitress came by to take their order. Mia ordered a bay shrimp salad to Adam's grilled salmon. A loaf of pumpernickel bread and cheesy biscuits were placed on the table along with garlic-infused butter. Mia's mouth watered. When Adam offered her the bread, she grabbed a cheesy biscuit.

"Hungry?"

"Starving."

"Dig in. So when does the baby eat?"

"She'll be fussing the minute my food arrives, I'm sure. She has an inner time clock that keeps Aunt Mia in shape. My hips are grateful."

"So am I." A wicked smile graced his face.

"Is that so?" She chuckled and didn't know what to make of Adam today. "Tell me that when it happens to you."

"I'm waiting for the day when Rose lets me feed her."

"The pediatrician said he might give me the okay to start feeding her solid foods. She might be eating with a spoon soon."

"So soon? I'll never get to feed her with a bottle."

"Yes, you will, Adam. She'll come around. And she'll be drinking from a bottle for a long time."

"I'd like to go to her next pediatrician's appointment with you. When is it?"

"Next week. I was going to ask you to join us, if you weren't too busy."

"I'm never going to be too busy for Rose," he said emphatically.

After their meals arrived, Mia got two bites of her salad in before the baby squawked and squirmed uncomfortably in her seat. "See, I told you. She has a sixth sense." She smiled at Rose. "You don't want your auntie Mia getting chubby, do you?"

"I'm recognizing her different cries now. That's definitely a hunger cry." He dug into the diaper bag and grabbed the bottle. He gave it a few shakes and handed it to her. "I wish she'd let me help you more."

Mia lifted the baby out of the infant seat. "You're welcome to try anytime you want, Adam." She gestured with the bottle.

"Not now. I wouldn't want to get kicked out of this place. The food is good. I'd like to come back."

"Chicken," Mia said, grinning. Rose was getting good at holding the smaller four-ounce bottles on her own. Mia fed the baby with one hand and picked up her fork and took bites of her salad with the other.

"You make it all work, Mia." Adam's note of admiration wasn't lost on her. "You multitask like a pro."

"Thanks. Are you buttering me up for something?"

He cut into his meal and chewed thoughtfully. "Why, because I'm paying you a compliment?"

"Well, yes. There is that."

"You caught me. But I'd give you the compliment even if I didn't have something to ask you."

"So, I was right?"

"Yes." He braced his arms on the table's edge and leaned forward, capturing her attention. "I want to take you and the baby away for the weekend."

"What?" She couldn't possibly have heard him correctly.

"I'm going to a wedding, and I want to take you with me."

She absorbed that for a moment. "You want me or the baby?"

"Both of you, of course."

Meaning, he wanted Rose with him, and the only way that could happen was if she went, too. They were a package deal.

"My friend is getting married, and you're both invited. It's in a small town in Texas. We'll leave Friday morning and be home by Sunday afternoon. It's short notice, but I'm hoping you'll say yes."

"I don't know, Adam." She began shaking her head. "Taking Mia on a plane can get complicated. I'd have to check it out with her doctor. Wouldn't it be easier for you to go without us?"

"I'm chartering one of my brother's planes. So we'd have a ton of room and all the conveniences we'd need. The trip is less than four hours, Mia. And well, I don't want to stall the small amount of progress I've made with Rose. The truth is, I don't want to miss a minute of time with her."

It was a tough situation. Mia was pretty much at his mercy. If he wanted to take his daughter somewhere, Mia would always be the tagalong. "Texas?"

"It'll be fun. A change of scenery. The wedding is being held in a barn on his property."

"Whose property?"

"Zane Williams."

Mia shrieked. "*The* Zane Williams. The country superstar?"

He nodded, blinking at her outburst.

"For heaven's sake, Adam. Don't you know any normal people?"

He chuckled. "Zane is as down-to-earth as they come. He's a great guy, and he wants to meet my daughter. Mia, I really want you there with me. It's not just about the baby."

Could she believe that? Should she trust him enough to believe he genuinely wanted her with him? "Give me some time to think about it."

"Okay. I can do that."

The meal was over, and Mia fastened Rose into her infant carrier again. Adam paid the check and picked up the carrier, inserting it into the stroller base. With a click, the baby was latched in. He was getting good with the baby's gadgets.

Adam assumed the position, taking hold of the stroller handle. "Ready, my pretty little Rose? Daddy's going to take you for a walk." She lagged behind as he strolled the baby out of the restaurant and onto the sidewalk, heading back to the shop.

There would be nothing left of her heart if Adam continued being so sweet and loving. He wanted to be a father in every sense of the word. How could she stand in his way?

She already knew what her answer to the weekend trip had to be.

She couldn't seem to deny Adam Chase anything anymore.

Ten

The plane trip was as comfortable as Adam said it would be. Rose slept most of the time in her car seat, and Mia and Adam played games with her during the rest of the trip. Mia had half hoped the pediatrician wouldn't give Rose permission to fly, but that hadn't been the case at all. Rose had gotten the all clear. And now Adam sat facing Mia in a stretch limo loaded down with baby equipment, heading toward Beckon, Texas.

"Tell me about Zane and his fiancée," Mia asked Adam, keeping her voice low. The baby's eyes were drifting closed again. Mia wished she could join her in a nap. "You told me that he'd leased the house next door to you and that you'd become friends during that time. But that's all I know, really."

Adam poured her a glass of lemonade from the bar and extended his arm to hand it her. "Thanks."

"You haven't read about it? It's big entertainment news. I guess the story got leaked out about Zane falling for his late wife's sister. They fell in love when Jessica came to Moonlight Beach to heal her wounds from being dumped at the altar."

"I don't have much time to read that stuff, Adam."

Adam poured himself a glass of lemonade, too, and took a sip. "Jessica is a nice woman. You're going to like her. She's a schoolteacher. I got to know her a bit when she lived here."

"And so will this wedding be a three-ring circus?"

"It shouldn't be. They were keeping their wedding plans a secret. Zane had rumors spread that they were hoping to get married next summer on the beach where they met. So, hopefully, this small farm wedding won't attract attention."

"I hope not, for their sake. They deserve to have a private ceremony."

His eyes flickered as he flashed a smile. That killer rare smile did things to her insides. Then he slid across from his seat to sit beside her and brought his hand up to her face. The gentle touch had her lifting her chin, and their eyes met as his arm wrapped around her shoulder. "I'm glad you're with me, Mia."

"Me, too," she said, taking a swallow of air.

His head bent toward her, and her mouth was captured in a long delicious kiss that was sweet, soothing and different from the way he'd kissed her before. "It's a long ride," he said. "Why don't you close your eyes and get some rest?"

It was just what she needed. The plane trip and all the preparations beforehand had worn her out. "Sounds perfect."

He cradled her in his arms and coaxed her head onto his chest. He smelled of musk and man, so strong and so good. The sound of his heart beating, the rapid thump, thump, thumping, calmed and comforted her as she drifted off.

A kiss to her forehead snapped her eyes wide-open. "Wake up, sweetheart."

Mia pushed up and away from Adam's grasp to get her bearings. The limo was parked in front of a hotel. All those miles of flatlands were behind them. "Did I sleep the whole way?"

"You and Rose were sleepyheads."

She gazed at Rose in the car seat. Her eyes were just now opening. "Wow, I didn't mean to sleep so long." She fiddled with her mussed hair. She must look a wreck.

"You needed the rest. You do a lot, holding down a job and taking care of Rose."

"I love it."

"I know, but that doesn't mean it doesn't wear you down at times."

She couldn't disagree. She'd been getting up with Rose twice a night the last few days. The baby was cutting teeth and wasn't sleeping through the night.

The chauffeur opened the door, and Adam unsnapped the baby out of the infant seat. He handed her off to Mia before she fussed and then extended his hand to help them out of the car. After Adam gave the driver instructions regarding the baby equipment, he guided her to the front desk and checked them into the only two-room suite on the premises.

Beckon wasn't a destination stop, but Zane Williams had put their little town on the map. He was their pride and joy. That much she knew about the country star.

As they entered the elevator, Adam whispered in her ear. "I can't promise you a five-star hotel. But I was assured it's a decent place."

"All I need are clean sheets and a nice bathtub and I'm happy."

"Is that all it takes to make you happy?"

"Uh-huh." She glanced at him. There was a lightness to Adam lately that kept her on her toes. "And what makes you happy?"

"Whatever makes you happy, Mia."

If he wanted her to jump his bones, he was halfway there. She liked this new Adam. He was charming and sweet. It sort of unsettled her, though. His abrupt turnaround seemed too good to be true.

"Right answer," she said as she stepped out of the elevator to face their suite.

Adam opened the door and they stepped inside. "Wow, this is nice," she said immediately. It was spacious with a flat-screen television on the wall and two lovely sofas facing a fireplace. A double door opened to one large bedroom and a master bath.

A large bouquet of pink lilies filled a glass-blown lavender vase that sat on the fireplace hearth. Adam walked over to it and read the card. "It's from Zane and Jessica, welcoming us to Beckon."

"Nice of them," she said. Rose was getting heavy in her arms. "Adam, can you lay a blanket down, please?"

He jumped to help her, retrieving the blanket from the diaper bag. Kneeling down, he placed it in the center of the room, and Mia met him there as she laid the baby down on her stomach. "Tummy time," she said. Then she gazed at Adam. "There's only one bedroom," she blurted. It was one of the first things she'd noticed about the suite.

"You and the baby take the bedroom. I'll sleep in here," he said. "I'm sure the sofas fold out into beds."

Their eyes locked, and warmth heated her cheeks. It was one thing living under Adam's roof in a huge mansion of sixteen rooms. A person could go all day without bumping into anyone else, but here? *Awkward.*

"You're pretty when you blush," Adam said.

Her shoulders slumped. No sense skirting the issue. "It's not as if we haven't slept together, Adam. But we have to be careful for Rose's sake that we don't make a mistake."

"I agree. We're on the same page, Mia."

"We are? Okay, good." As long as she made herself clear. Adam had no clue how hard it would be to go to bed tonight knowing he was only steps away. She wasn't as immune to him as she pretended, especially lately. He'd been a dream these past few days. "So what's on the agenda today?" she asked.

"Well, first we take a little rest and get settled. And later tonight there's a welcome barbecue at the farm. Zane's in the process of building Jessica a house, so it'll be on his property, but prepare to rough it a bit."

"You didn't design the house by any chance?"

"It's their wedding present. Zane had specifics and I helped him along."

"It's probably going to be fantastic, a dream home."

"I hope so."

"If you designed it, it will be."

Adam's expression softened and warmth filled his eyes. "Thank you."

She stared at him. "You're welcome."

Their luggage arrived at the door, breaking the moment, and they spent the next twenty minutes unpacking and setting up the baby's equipment.

By six o'clock they were standing on Zane Williams's property, a vast amount of land accented by cottonwoods and lush meadows. Off in the distance, she saw the house under construction and could only imagine how beautiful it would be when it was done. Adam told her there were balconies and terraces to the rear of the home facing a lake.

The party invitation had said ultracasual. Mia wore a soft cotton paisley dress and tall tan leather boots. Adam told her she looked very much like a country girl. Adam did the cowboy thing justice, too. He wore jeans, a belt buckle, boots and a black Western shirt with white snaps. He could easily play the sexy villain in a Western movie in that getup.

"Ready?" he asked.

She nodded and Adam placed a hand to her back as they headed on foot toward the festivities held under tall thick oaks shading the area. Mia pushed the stroller, and when the terrain got a little too rough, Adam took over. As they approached a set of picnic benches with candles burning and vases filled with willowy wildflowers dotting the length of the dressed tables, intense hickory scents flavored the air and worked at her appetite. Beyond the benches, smoke billowed from three giant smoker barbecue grills.

"Howdy," said a voice she recognized. She owned at

least three of Zane Williams's albums. And sure enough, he was approaching them, holding the hand of a pretty blonde woman. "Adam, I'm glad you could make it. Congratulations on being a daddy."

The men shook hands and the woman placed a kiss on Adam's cheek. "Yes and congrats from me, too, neighbor. So glad you all made it for our wedding."

"I am, too, Jess. You're looking beautiful and very happy," Adam said.

She winked. "Never could pull the wool over your eyes, Adam. And who are these gorgeous ladies?"

Adam made the introductions. Mia couldn't believe Zane Williams actually gave her a warm hug and thanked her for coming. "Nice meeting you and congratulations. Little Rose, is she?"

"Yes, she was named after my mother," she told the couple.

"Pretty name," Zane said, crouching down to get a better look at Rose. "She's got your eyes, Adam. Such a pretty little thing."

"And you're the baby's aunt?" Jessica asked softly, eyeing the baby.

"Yes, I'm Aunt Mia." There was no need to go into further detail. She didn't know how much Adam had told them, but she was certain it wasn't all that much.

"Well, I hope you have a nice time this evening," Zane said. "We've invited our closest friends and family. Before we eat, we'll go around and introduce you to everyone."

"Sounds good," Adam said.

Mia raised her brows. There must be fifty people in attendance. Small for wedding standards, but would Adam make the rounds to meet everyone or stay in the shadows like he always did?

"Would you like to sit down?" Adam asked after Jessica and Zane left. "Looks like we can take our pick of seats."

"Actually, I'd like to walk around a bit. If you don't mind trudging around with the stroller."

"Not at all." They headed away from the festivities, staying to flat grounds, Rose cooing and gurgling as they bumped along a grassy path. "I didn't know Rose was named after your mother."

"She was. Rose was her middle name."

"Makes me wonder what else I don't know about you. And don't say, welcome to my world."

Mia's breath caught. At some point, she'd wanted to tell Adam about her life and share her innermost secrets. But did she know him well enough? So far the men in her life had only disappointed her. If Adam hurt her, she'd be devastated. She'd wait for the time when Adam met her halfway. Right now, he already knew much more about her than she knew about him. "How about, welcome to my universe?"

"Very funny, Mia." But Adam was smiling, and he didn't press her.

They walked along in silence and returned in time to meet Zane and Jessica's family and friends. All the while, Adam stayed by her side and was cordial to everyone, shaking hands, making small talk.

They sat down to the best barbecue Mia had ever eaten. She tasted a little of everything. The spareribs were to die for. The corn on the cob smoked in their husks and flavored with honey butter, insane. The chicken, shrimp and brisket were all tender and tasty. Mia had never eaten so much in her life.

Zane and Jess sat down with them after the meal. Mia was enamored by the love they shared. Zane's eyes gleamed when he looked at his fiancée and spoke about the house they'd live in and the children they hoped to have one day. Mia's heart did a little tumble. How lovely to see two people so blessed by love. Her mother had never had that. And Mia's track record with the opposite sex wasn't all

THE BILLIONAIRE'S DADDY TEST

that good, either. She'd met too many men like her father. Flakes, liars or losers. She'd weeded out quite a few, and what was left in the dating pool hadn't been all that inspiring.

From under the table, Adam's hand sought hers and he entwined their fingers. It seemed like such a natural move and yet it meant something monumental. She glanced at his strong profile as he bantered with Zane and clung on to her hand, his thumb absently stroking over her skin.

Sweet, amazing sensations whipped through her. Somehow, after their arguments, their intense lovemaking and their time spent with Rose, after pranking those teens on the beach, kissing under the moonlight and holding hands under the table, Mia had fallen fully and deeply in love with Adam Chase.

She loved him. There wasn't anything she could do about it.

She'd put up a good battle. She'd tried to talk herself out of it. She'd tried to keep her distance, falling short of her goal a time or two, but it was no use. Adam wasn't a flake, a liar or a loser. He was pretty wonderful. And she was about to give him the one thing she hadn't given another man. Her full trust.

"Well, it's time for me to punish y'all with a song or two," Zane was saying. The sun had set and glass lights slung from tree to tree lit the night. "We've got a fire going. Come on around to the fire pit and bring the baby, too. I'll sing her a lullaby."

"I'll round up our guests," Jess said "Mia, I'll come sit with you in a while."

"I'd like that."

Adam helped her up and gave her a kiss on the cheek. "What was that for?"

"Just because," he said and squeezed her hand before he let her go.

Could he be feeling the same sentiment and mood as

her? Was being outdoors under the stars with all the talk of love and marriage getting to him?

With darkness came cooler breezes, and Mia shivered a bit. "Rose is going to need a sweater," she said.

"I'm right on it." Adam reached into the basket under the stroller and gave her a choice of a blue knit sweater or a black-and-pink sequined Hello Kitty jacket.

"Such a good daddy."

"Unless you think it's too cold for the baby," he added. "If you want to head back to the hotel, I'm fine with it."

"And miss a private performance by Zane Williams? Not on your life." She nabbed the jacket out of his hands.

Adam laughed.

It was such a beautiful sound.

Adam laid the sleeping baby into the play yard, her own personal bed brought from home. Mia loved the way he handled Rose now, confident but also so tenderly it made her heart sing. Standing together in the hotel bedroom, they watched her take peaceful breaths. Adam reached for Mia's hand again, and their fingers naturally entwined. She could stay this way forever, in the quiet of the night, with the man she loved and their little bundle of sweetness.

"The party knocked her out," Adam said.

"It's been a long day."

"Are you tired? Should I leave you, so you can get some sleep?"

"No, stay." The night had been perfect and she didn't want it to end.

"Let's have a drink." He lingered one more second over Rose and then led her into the living room. "Have a seat," he said, leaving her by the sofa. "I'll get us something from the bar."

Instead Mia walked over to him and laid her hand on his arm. "Adam, I don't need a drink."

He turned to her, his brows lifting. "You don't?"

She shook her head. "I don't," she said softly, staring into his eyes.

His lids lowered, and his arms wrapped around her waist. "What do you want, sweetheart?" he rasped.

Mia rose up on tiptoes and pressed her lips to his. She'd taken him momentarily by surprise, but Adam was fast on his feet, and she loved that about him. He drew her up, cradling her body to his, deepening the kiss and letting her know with deep-throated groans that he wanted her as much as she wanted him.

Their kisses led to the shedding of their clothes and the two of them falling onto the sofa cushions. Adam's hands roved her body, his touches eliciting white-hot sensations that brought her to the brink of ecstasy. She cried out quietly, muting her sighs with closed lips. Adam was an expert at drawing her out. And when he coaxed her to do the same to him, she didn't disappoint. Her caresses led to bolder moves as she explored his body and made love to him in every way she knew how.

She gave him her whole self, holding nothing back. Making love on a sofa brought out Adam's inventive side. He positioned her in ways that heated her blood and made her ache for more. Mia was happy, so happy she didn't want to think about where this would lead. She shut her mind off to anything but good thoughts and as she climbed higher and higher, Adam wringing out every last ounce of her energy, each powerful thrust brought her closer to completion. And then it happened. His name tumbled from her lips over and over and her body splintered.

Adam wasn't far behind, and as he held her, his face inches from hers, his eyes locked on hers, he bucked his body one last time and shed a release that brought them both earth-shattering pleasure.

He collapsed on top of her, and she bore his weight. Her hands played in his sweat-moistened hair as his mouth found hers. His kiss was gentler now, easy and loving. "Are you okay, sweetheart?" he murmured.

"Mmm." She was humming inside, feeling wonderful, filled with love.

Adam rolled off her, taking her with him so she wouldn't fall off the sofa. It was a tight fit, but there wasn't anywhere she'd rather be. "Mia, we're good together." He kissed her forehead.

It was hardly a declaration of love, but if it was the best he had to offer, she'd take it. "We are."

A cool blast of air made her shiver. It was hard to believe since Adam's body was a hot furnace. But the air conditioner was running and the room was growing chilly.

"You're cold?"

"A little."

"Let me get the sofa bed ready, Mia. I want you with me tonight. Will you stay?"

"I'll stay."

"Good." She was lifted off him and kissed soundly on the lips. "You go check on Rose. I'll only be a minute."

She grabbed Adam's shirt, fitting her arms through the sleeves and scooted out of the room. The baby was still peaceful and sleeping on her back, her cheeks as rosy as ever, such a pretty sight. She was plenty warm in her sleep sack.

When she returned to the room, the bed was made up and Adam was waiting. He patted the spot beside him and she climbed in next to him. The back of the sofa as their headboard, they used pillows to prop up. Adam put his arm around her shoulders and she snuggled in, bringing a sheet over them. "Better?" he asked.

"Much. The baby is still asleep."

He kissed her forehead. "I haven't been this happy in a long time."

She let those words sink in. "Since when, Adam?"

He was silent for a while. Had he been thinking out

loud? Did he regret revealing that much to her and had she overstepped again, trying to get information out of him? He let go a deep sigh, and her breath caught. Then he spoke. "I was almost engaged once. I thought we were perfect together. Her name was Jacqueline."

"What happened with her?" she asked in a whisper.

"She broke it off. Pretty much broke my heart. I thought we were crazy in love, but it turned out I'd been wrong about our relationship. I'd never been poleaxed like that before. You know, it was like a sucker punch to my gut."

"I'm so sorry, Adam."

"That's not all. About a month later, I called her. It was late at night and I couldn't sleep. I'd been rehashing everything and it all seemed so wrong. I thought surely she was having doubts about the breakup. It was all a big mistake. I can still remember the shock I felt when I heard my brother's voice on the other end of the phone. For a few seconds, it didn't quite click. I thought I'd dialed the wrong number. And when it hit me, my head nearly exploded. I'm surprised I didn't grind my teeth to the bone. Of course, Brandon made all sorts of excuses, but he didn't deny the fact that he and Jacqueline were together."

"Oh, Adam. Really? Brandon and Jacqueline? That was the ultimate betrayal."

"I thought so. Believe me—I wasn't happy with either one of them. I didn't speak to Brandon until they broke up three years later. He cheated on her, and she finally wised up and dumped him."

"Wow. So that's what you have against him. I get it now. You must've loved her a lot."

"It was years ago, Mia. I'm over her, and Brandon is who he is. My mother has been after me for years to mend fences. Somehow it's my fault all of this happened. She believes Brandon didn't go after Jacqueline until after she broke up with me. I can't blame Mom. She wants us to be close like we once were."

"What happened is clearly not your fault," Mia said. "But you have forgiven your brother, haven't you?"

"There's a difference between forgiving and forgetting. I'm not holding a grudge. But I can't forget who Brandon is."

"Is that why you warned me about him?"

She set her hand on his chest and stroked him tenderly, sliding over his skin, hoping to soothe him, calm him, make the pain go away. He reached for her hand and lifted it to his lips, placing a kiss on her palm. They were finally connecting, finally making headway.

"If he goes anywhere near you, there's no telling what I'd do to him."

Warmth spiraled through her body, a slow flow of heat that surrounded her entirely. "You don't have to worry— there's only one Chase I'm interested in." She kissed his shoulder, and he gazed into her eyes. There was no mistaking the gratitude and relief she found in them.

"I'm glad." He sighed heavily as if relieved of his burden. "I feel like I've been given a second chance with my life. I don't want to blow it again."

"Adam, what do you mean, second chance? Are you talking about your sister? Is it about Lily?"

His eyes closed then, as if the pain was too much. He shook his head. "Yes, but I can't talk about Lily now, Mia. I can't talk about my sister."

"Okay." There was enough force in his voice to make her a believer. "You don't have to tell me."

"Thank you, sweetheart."

Adam was trying. It was all she could ask of him.

The old barn was decorated with wildflowers, lilies and white roses. Sprays of color splashed over haystacks, and snowy sheer curtains were draped from rafter to rafter overhead. Hundreds of flameless candles cast romantic lighting over the entire interior of the barn and lanterns on pickets defined each row of white satin chairs tied with big bows.

"It's beautiful," Mia said. She sat beside him in the last row. A precaution, she'd said, in case the baby fussed, she could duck out and make a quick escape.

"*You're* beautiful," he whispered. "The place is okay."

The jade in her eyes brightened, and he winked playfully. Mia wore a stunning pastel-pink dress that met her waist in delicate folds, accented her sexy hips and flowed to her knees. Her hair was down and curled, and her olive skin absolutely glowed. Rose looked cute as a button. She wore pink, too, her dress a mass of fancy ruffles. A big matching bow wrapped around her forehead. She was smiling now, her eyes gleaming as she took in the candles and colorful flowers surrounding her.

Adam knew a sense of peace. This moment in time couldn't be more perfect. He reached for Mia's hand— he'd been doing that lately, sometimes without realizing it—and held it on his knee.

Violins began to play, and people milling about promptly took their seats.

Zane appeared, walking in from the side entrance, wearing tuxedo tails and his signature cowboy hat, looking happier than he'd ever seen him. Zane took his place next to the minister at the back of the barn. A ray of sunshine poured over him from the loft window—he had his own personal spotlight—as he searched the aisle for signs of his bride.

And then the orchestra kicked up, playing a classic version of "Here Comes the Bride."

A hush fell over the barn.

Jessica stepped up and all eyes turned toward her. Chairs creaked and shuffling sounds echoed against the walls as everyone rose to their feet.

"I love her dress," Mia whispered.

Ivory and satin, with lace everywhere, Jessica made a lovely bride.

She'd been jilted at the altar once before, but if Adam knew Zane, he was more than going to make up for that.

Jessica made her trip down the aisle, smiling, her face beaming, the bouquet of star lilies and gardenias trembling in her hands.

She reached Zane, and everyone settled back into their seats.

The minister gave a lovely speech about second chances, and something hit home for Adam as he reached for Mia's hand again. He'd liked waking up with her this morning. Almost as much as he'd enjoyed taking her to bed last night. And afterward, he'd managed to give her a glimpse into his life. He'd told her things about Brandon and Jacqueline he'd never shared before with another human being. He'd shared his heartache with her, the betrayal that ruined him for love.

He'd been over Jacqueline for a long time. But he'd never get over Lily. Mia hadn't pressed him last night about her, and he'd been relieved. He kept those memories buried.

Rose began to kick in her infant seat. She had a shelf life of about twenty minutes, before things got out of hand. Her complaints started quietly and Mia took out a long-necked giraffe teething toy. She handed it to Rose, and that seemed to settle her.

Zane and Jessica exchanged vows, making mention of the woman they'd both loved and lost, Janie Holcomb Williams, and promised to do her memory honor by living a good and happy life. Adam had never met Zane's first wife, but he knew the heartache her death had caused to both Jessica and Zane. It was a touching moment, and even Mia shed a tear or two.

Now the minister was asking if anyone knew a reason why the couple shouldn't be joined in holy matrimony, and Rose's mouth opened as if on cue. A belch blasted from her lips, so loud it was hard to believe the uncouth sound had come from such a tiny person.

The entire assembly laughed. Zane and Jessica glanced over their shoulders and chuckled, too.

Mia gasped and looked at Adam in wide-eyed shock, but then a slow grin spread across her face and they both burst out laughing, like everyone else.

The minister made a joke about that not counting, garnering a few more chuckles and he proceeded with the ceremony.

After the wedding, the barn was transformed into a reception hall. The orchestra was replaced by Zane's country band, and a dance floor was laid down. Appetizers were passed around and a bar was set up. It all flowed smoothly.

Mia had the baby out of the infant carrier now and was swaying to the music. Rose was cackling, making those little sounds of happiness that ripped into his heart. He wound his arms around both of them, Rose sandwiched in between, and swayed with them, rocking back and forth to the music. It seemed as long as Mia was present, his finicky little daughter would tolerate him.

"Now that's a sight to behold."

Adam turned to the smiling groom. "Hey, buddy. Congratulations." He shook his hand and gave him a light slap on the back. "Great ceremony."

"Thanks. Thanks. We did it. Jess is a beautiful bride, isn't she?"

"She is." Mia stepped up to give him a hug. "Congratulations. I feel honored to have been invited."

"Hey, well, you and this little one are part of Adam's family now." Zane smiled and playfully wiggled Rose's toes. "She even participated in the ceremony."

Mia's gaze shot up. "Oh, gosh. I'm sorry about the disruption. You never know what these little ones are going to do. Leave it to Rose to make her presence known," she said.

"She's a glutton for attention. She doesn't get that from me," Adam said.

"Oh, so you're saying it comes from my side of the family," Mia teased.

"Hey, we didn't mind. Honestly," Zane said.

"Not at all," Jessica said as she joined Zane, slipping her hand in his. "It was just what the ceremony needed, a little levity."

Jessica's appearance brought another round of hugs and congratulations. And shortly after, the announcement was made that dinner was ready.

Halfway through the meal, Adam's phone vibrated. He pulled it out of his pocket and frowned when he saw the name lit up on the screen. He wanted to ignore the call and finish his meal with Mia, but something told him he needed to answer his brother's call. He kissed Mia's cheek, breathing in her intoxicating scent and rose. "Excuse me. I've got to take this call. Are you going to be all right?"

"We'll be fine. Rose needs a diaper change. I was just about to take her."

"Okay, I'll meet you back here and we'll finish our meal."

He walked out of the barn and strode toward the construction site, away from the music and conversations and picked up on the fifth ring. "Brandon, it's Adam. I'm at a wedding in Texas. What's up?"

"Adam. You need to come home right away. Mom's had a heart attack."

Eleven

Adam held his mother's pasty hand, gazing into her soft blue eyes. A pallor had taken over her skin as she lay in the hospital bed. She was hooked up to IV tubes and oxygen, yet she managed to smile. "Hi, Mom."

"Adam, you came." Her voice was weak.

"Of course I came." He squeezed her hand. He'd flown half the night to get back to Los Angeles, hoping he wouldn't be too late. He'd had a limo waiting at the airport and had come first thing. Mia and the baby were driven to Grandma Tess's home so she could spend time with Rose.

"I'm so glad you both are here," Mom said, glancing at Brandon, too.

Brandon stepped up. "Of course we're here."

"I'm sorry to worry you. I don't know what happened. One minute I was fine, shopping with Ginny, and the next thing I know, my legs went out from under me. I felt terribly weak, and a few kind people at the mall brought me over to a bench and sat me down. Someone called nine-one-one."

"I'm glad they did. You need to be here," Brandon said. He'd been in constant contact with Adam, letting him know the status of the tests they were doing. "Mom, you've had a bad attack of angina. It's not life-threatening, but you do have to take it easier now. Eat better, watch your diet. You'll probably be put on medication, too."

"They're keeping me here for a few days."

"Just for observation," Brandon said. "They've got a few more tests to run, and they want to monitor you. I think it's a good idea."

"I do, too," Adam said, greatly relieved the emergency wasn't more serious. He wasn't ready to say goodbye to his mother.

Tears filled her eyes. "I was shopping for Rose. Oh dear... I want to see her grow up, Adam. I want to be around for all of it."

"You will, Mom." She didn't get to see her own daughter grow up. She didn't have the chance to raise Lily. "You'll see Rose as much as you want. I'll make sure of it, Mom. I'll be sure to keep my baby safe." His voice cracked. Fatigue, worry and regret had him spilling out words he'd always wanted to say. Words that he'd harbored for years. "I won't let you down the way I did with Lily."

"Oh no...you didn't... Please don't feel that way. I don't blame you. I never did, son. And that was before Brandon told me the truth earlier today." Her face tightened, the wrinkles around her eyes creasing.

Adam whipped his head around. "Brandon, what did you tell her?"

"The truth, Adam," his brother said. His jaw tight, the hard rims of his eyes softened. "I told Mom about how you covered for me during that storm. How you wanted to leave the storm cellar and check for Lily and how I lied to you. I told you Lily was with Mom, when I knew it wasn't true. I was too scared to let you go looking for her up at the house. I didn't want you to leave me alone. You were my big brother and I needed you to protect me." Brandon put his head down.

Adam let that sink in. Seconds ticked by, his mind scrambling for answers. "Why now?" he asked Brandon.

"Because he thought I was dying, Adam."

He stared at his mother. Then blinked. She'd shocked him, but her expression now was solid and more alive than

when he'd first walked into her room. "It's been bother-
ing him for years—isn't that what you said, Brandon? And
today you thought I might die before you could confess
the truth to me."

"Mom, you're not dying." His brother's voice was deep
and compassionate.

"From your lips to God's ears." Her pained sigh re-
sounded in the quiet room. Her head against her bed pillows, she closed her eyes. "The truth is, I've been blaming
myself all these years. I shouldn't have left Lily alone with
you boys." Her voice was soft, reverent and full of regret.
She peered at both of them. "She was only six. You were
twelve, Adam, and Brandon was eight. I knew we lived in
tornado country. It was to be a quick trip to the grocery
store, but I should've taken Lily with me. She wasn't your
responsibility—she was mine. I'm more to blame than anyone. I'm only grateful, when that tornado ripped through
our land, you boys didn't die along with her. Adam, you
took your brother to safety and kept him there. Or maybe
all three of you would've died."

Brandon had tears in his eyes. "I told Adam I saw Lily
go in the car with you, so he wouldn't leave me alone. I
lied, and Lily died."

"You were so young, Brandon," Mom said. "I understand how scared you must've been. But have you ever
once considered that you might have saved both of your
lives that day?"

"No, Mom, I never did. And I've hated myself ever
since." Brandon spoke quietly, his voice nearly breaking.

Adam winced and breathed deep, keeping his emotions
at bay. He couldn't break down now. He couldn't show the
world, or his family, his vulnerability, yet the scars within
him were on fire. He was burning and didn't know how to
stop it.

He'd never known Brandon felt guilty about Lily's death.
They'd never spoken of it. Adam had always blamed him-

self for not seeing through Brandon's lies, for not knowing his little brother had been too frightened to let him go after Lily. He was older, the responsible one when his mother wasn't around. He should've checked on his sister regardless of what Brandon told him. But often he questioned whether he would've actually taken those steps up from the storm cellar even if Brandon hadn't stopped him. He'd been afraid, too; the noises outside had been horrifying. Adam had always wished he would've done something different. Been stronger. Acted braver.

His head pounded. All these years, he'd resented Brandon and had been more than willing to hate his brother when he'd discovered his involvement with Jacqueline, but now... He wasn't sure about anything.

"I'm sorry, Adam," Brandon said, his face flushed. He was trying valiantly to hold back tears.

It was a genuine, heartfelt apology. He never thought he'd hear those words from Brandon, and in the course of a few weeks, he'd heard them twice.

"I've let you carry this burden all these years. The truth is, I think I intentionally sabotaged my relationship with Jacqueline because I knew I didn't deserve her and because I'd hurt you. I've been a coward. About everything."

Adam swallowed.

"I know you've despised me. I can't blame you, Adam. But I'm apologizing for all I've done that has hurt you."

"I don't despise you, Brandon."

"You boys were always fighting," his mother said. "But I knew back then, just as I know now, you love each other. So shake hands once and for all. Heaven knows there's enough guilt in this room to feed the devil. The past has hurt all of us. It's time to move on."

They looked at each other now, and the hope and apology in Brandon's eyes had Adam extending his hand. Brandon clasped it. "You're a good man, Adam. Always have been."

He nodded, too choked up to speak.

The nurse walked in. "Excuse me, but you have another visitor," she said to his mom. "But I'm afraid we can allow only two visitors at a time. One of you will have to leave."

Mia stood at the door, holding a vase of spring flowers. "Is it okay?"

Adam gazed at Mia. She was a bright and wonderful light shining through all of his past darkness.

"I'll leave, so you three can spend time together." Brandon offered. He walked to the door and gave Mia a kiss on the cheek. "Thanks for coming," he said and walked out of sight.

"I don't want to interrupt," she said to Adam, still not moving.

And it hit him, just like that. He *wanted* her there. He needed her support. Especially after the conversation he'd just had with Brandon. She'd come, and that meant a lot to him. "Please, come in."

"Yes," his mother said quietly. "It's good to see you, dear."

"I was worried about you, Alena," Mia said, walking into the room. Adam took the flowers and placed them on a small table under the television where his mother could see them easily.

"The flowers are lovely," his mother said. "Thank you."

"I was hoping you'd enjoy them," Mia said.

"Mia, I'm sorry to interrupt your plans with my son this weekend. I feel awful about that."

"Don't think of it. Your health is important to us. You've just got to concentrate on getting better." Mia reached for her hand. "How are you feeling now?"

"Better. It was frightening, I will admit. I had an angina attack that knocked me for a loop. I have to stay a day or two for monitoring, but then I'll be going home."

"That's great news," Mia said, her eyes so beautifully hopeful.

"Where is Rose today?"

"My grandma Tess is watching her for a few hours."

"That's nice. I hope you'll let me babysit one day, too."

"I'm sure you will."

"Come sit and tell me all about the trip. How did Rose do at the wedding?"

Mia lowered down on the edge of the bed. "Well, uh…" Her eyes met his, and they shared a conspiratorial moment. Little Rose was the maker of many stories, and this one would surely bring a smile to his mother's face. She could use a little levity. The last few minutes had been laden with grief, guilt and regret.

Adam breathed a sigh of relief, taking a step back, allowing Mia to comfort his mother.

"She did fine, except for this one moment during the ceremony…"

The next day, Mia walked through the door lugging Mia in her infant seat in one arm and a file folder she'd brought from First Clips tucked under the other arm. Since the wedding and Alena's health scare she wanted to work from home more these days, to be closer to Adam. Rose had a way of cheering him up, even if she still wasn't too keen on him. Adam adored being with her. And one day soon, his daughter would come to accept him. Every day together brought them closer and closer. Mia sensed that Rose was warming to him.

She was heading upstairs to her room, when she spotted a young woman sitting on the living room sofa speaking with Mary. She set down her files on the entry table and unfastened the straps of the carrier, lifting Rose into her arms. "Let's see what's going on," she said, kissing the baby's forehead. The baby gurgled, and Mia's heart warmed. Casually, her curiosity getting the better of her, she strolled into the living room.

"Hi, Mary. We're home," she said.

The woman popped up from her seat immediately and

turned to her. The spunky blonde was all smiles as her gaze locked on to the baby. "This must be the little dar-lin', Rose."

One glance at Mary's sheepish expression sent dread to her belly. "Hello, Mia."

Mia waited, staring at the woman who couldn't be more than twenty-two.

"Mia D'Angelo, this is Lucille Bridges," Mary said. "She's from Nanny Incorporated."

"I have an appointment with Adam Chase this afternoon," the woman added.

Nanny Incorporated? Adam had called a nanny agency? The blood in her veins boiled. The girl wouldn't take her eyes off Rose. Mia hugged her tighter and stepped back.

"I was just explaining to Miss Bridges that Adam isn't home. He must've forgotten about his appointment with all the commotion this past week. I've called him, but he hasn't answered his phone."

"He's at the hospital visiting his mother." She eyed the girl cautiously. "I'm sure he won't be home for quite a while."

"That's okay. I understand. I've left my references with Mary. I've been with the agency for three years and I have impeccable referrals," she said.

Wow, three whole years.

"Do you think I can say hello to the baby while I'm here?"

Mia's nerves jumped. She shot a glance at Mary.

"Uh, I think Aunt Mia was just about to put Rose down for a nap. It's past her naptime, isn't it, Mia?"

"Right," she gritted out. How could Adam do this to her? "Rose is quite a handful when she's tired."

"I know how babies can be. I helped raise four siblings."

Mia couldn't take it another second. Adam's betrayal and deceit didn't sit well in her gut. "I'm sure Mary can show you out. I've got to take the baby upstairs now."

"Oh, uh, sure. Bye-bye, Rose. Nice meeting you, Mia."

She headed for the stairs without responding.

She couldn't. Her throat had closed up.

She was in shock.

Trembling, she stood in the kitchen doorway, watching Adam forage through the refrigerator. It was after seven, and he'd just come home.

"I asked Mary to go home early," she said.

Adam backed up and peeked at her. "Good idea. I see she left us dinner." He pulled out covered dishes and set them on the counter. Lifting a lid, he said, "Looks like we're having rosemary chicken and—" he lifted the next lid "—glazed carrots."

"I won't be having dinner…w-with you." Her darn throat constricted again. Her anger had never subsided; neither did the hurt. She'd cried and cried all afternoon. Like a fool.

Adam stopped what he was doing to really look at her. "Why, sweetheart?" He approached her. "You're pale as a ghost. Are you feeling sick?"

He wrapped his arms around her, and for one instant, she relished it, squeezed her eyes closed and sought the pleasure of him, before she set both hands on his chest and shoved with all her might. Surprise more than force made him stumble back, his eyes wide and confused. "Yes, I'm sick, Adam. Of you. And all your secrets, lies and deceit. When were you going to tell me you were hiring a nanny for Rose? Were you going to hire someone, then toss me out onto the street? Was that your plan all along?"

Adam's tanned face flushed with color instantly. "Mia, for goodness' sake, calm the hell down."

"No, Adam. I will not calm down," she shouted. "How do you think I felt coming home to find a blonde bimbo nanny sitting on the couch, waiting for you?"

"Mia," he said, exasperated. "I meant to speak to you

about it. But then Mom had her attack and it slipped my mind."

"It slipped your mind!" Mia was one step away from losing it entirely. "It should've never *been* on your mind. Do you think I can't care for Rose? Am I lacking in some way? Or has the recluse in you decided that I'm getting too close, invading your precious privacy?" She gestured an air check with her index finger. "Checked me right off, didn't you?"

"No, of course not!"

She folded her arms. "I don't believe you."

"Shh, Mia, keep your voice down. Where's Rose?" he asked.

"Sleeping upstairs." She grabbed the monitor attached to her belt and showed him. "Regardless of what you might think of me, I'd never put Rose in danger. See, I'm watching her. She's my baby, too, Adam. You had no right. No right, going behind my back like that."

"Mia." His voice was an impatient rasp. "I know you'd never put Rose in danger. And if you'll let me explain what I was thinking."

"Apparently, you weren't thinking. Adam, that girl was a kid. I don't care that she claimed to have impeccable references—she doesn't know Rose, not the way I do."

Adam walked to the bar at the end of the huge granite counter and slapped a shot glass down. He filled it with vodka and downed it in one gulp. He didn't hesitate to pour a second shot.

"Alcohol never solved any problems, Adam."

He gulped the second shot and poured a third. "Don't lecture me, Mia. I won't get behind the wheel of my car and slaughter some poor innocent girl."

Mia froze. The swirling tirade in her head ready to lash out of her mouth vanished. She hadn't heard right, had she? "What?"

He slugged back the third shot and hunkered down, bracing his elbows on the counter. "Nothing."

"It was something, Adam." She walked over to him and spoke to his profile. "How do you know about that?"

"Know what?" He refused to look at her. It wasn't a coincidental statement. Adam Chase didn't leave things up to chance.

"About my father."

Silence.

"Adam, if you care one iota about me, you'll tell me how you know that right this minute."

Silence again.

Adam didn't care. Maybe he never had. She was through with Adam Chase. He would never let her in, never trust her. She turned her back on him and walked away. She was almost out of the kitchen when his voice broke the silence.

"I had you investigated."

A gasp exploded from her mouth. She whirled around. "You did what?"

He turned to face her. His expression was coarse, his eyes raw, not filled with the apology she'd expected. "I didn't know a thing about you, Mia. And when you came to me with that story about your sister and Rose, I didn't know if I could believe a word out of your mouth. After all the lies you'd told me when we first met, I had to find out more about you. I had to know who was coming to live in my house and help raise my daughter."

"You didn't trust me to tell you the truth."

"No, I didn't."

"I would have one day, Adam. I was waiting for you to open up to me. But I see that will never happen." She sighed, the conversation sapping her strength. "So, you know everything?"

He nodded.

Shame washed over her. She was the young Burkel girl again, whose father had mowed down a young teenager, a girl who'd had a full life yet to live. He'd been drunk, coming home from a scandalous affair with a married woman. The town scorned the Burkels. She couldn't go anywhere without being harassed or whispered about. It was equally painful going to school. Young Scarlett Brady, the victim, had been a classmate and the daughter of a revered police captain. Everyone knew and loved Scarlett. When her mother decided to move them to Grandma Tess's home, their neighbors put up balloons in celebration on the day they'd moved out. The memory brought fresh shivers.

"You didn't even tell me your real name, Mia. What was I to think?"

He'd had her investigated like a common criminal. She cringed at the thought. How so like Adam, though. Sweeping heartache invaded her from top to bottom. "That maybe I didn't lead a charmed life. That maybe my family suffered and we'd paid a big price for my father's deeds. That maybe I make mistakes, unlike you."

"I make mistakes, Mia."

"Yes, you're right. *This* was a big mistake. But that doesn't make what you've done any easier to take."

Adam wadded up the note Mia had left for him on the kitchen table that morning. She needed time to think, away from him. She had taken Rose with her, but she'd call often and let him know how Rose was doing. She'd be at her grandma Tess's home for the next few days. He was welcome to come visit her anytime. And please, don't call the police—she hadn't kidnapped his daughter.

What the hell. He'd never accuse her of kidnapping. That last part really gutted him through and through. Mia would never allow any harm to come to his daughter. He trusted Mia with Rose and knew he wasn't equipped to take care of the baby on his own. Not yet. Not like Mia could. He missed the both of them, like crazy.

Adam tossed the note, missing the trash can in his

office, and rubbed his temples. He had a headache that wouldn't let up. How had he thought he'd get any work done today? It was a foolish notion. Mia had called him twice already today with an update about Rose. She'd eaten a good breakfast. She'd pooped her diaper. She'd taken her for a walk around the neighborhood with her grandmother this morning.

"When are you coming home?" Adam had asked.

"I don't know, Adam," she'd replied coolly. The aloof tone of her voice worried him.

He knew when she did come home, nothing would be the same.

"Adam, Brandon's here," Mary announced at his doorway. "He's waiting for you downstairs."

"It's about damn time," he said, bounding up from his desk. "Thanks, Mary."

He strode down the stairs to find Brandon in the living room with a drink in his hand, a whiskey. He'd also had a tumbler of vodka ready for him. "So, Mia's gone?" Brandon held out the glass to him.

He should refuse the drink. Last night, he'd nearly polished off half a bottle and his head still throbbed. "Just one." He took it from his brother and nodded. "Yeah, she's gone."

"Let's sit outside, Adam. It's a cool afternoon. It'll help clear your head."

"Is that what I need?"

"Oh, I think so, brother." He led the way outside, where breezes took away the heat of the day. The sun, lowering on the horizon, cast a brilliant gleam on the water. "I have to say, I was surprised to get your call."

Adam shrugged. He was surprised he'd called his brother, too. Just went to show how crazy confused he was right now. "We might as well start behaving like brothers."

"You had no one else to call," Brandon stated and then sat down on a lounge chair.

Adam chuckled, taking a seat, as well. "Okay, guilty." He really didn't confide in anyone about personal matters. Trusting his brother didn't come easy, but Mia and Rose were important to him and oddly, he believed Brandon could help him sort this out. "You know women, Brandon. And you know me."

"I'm glad to help, bro. Go on. Tell me what happened with Mia."

"All of it?"

"Everything. I'm no relationship expert, but I've made enough mistakes now that I've gotten pretty good at rectifying them. And, yes, I do know women."

Adam spelled it out for Brandon. Telling him exactly how he'd met Mia on the beach. Explaining Rose's negative reaction to him and how Mia coming to live with him had been necessary, at least in the beginning. He recounted the past few weeks, up to a point.

"Have you slept with her?" Brandon asked.

"Why does that matter?" Adam shot back.

"Just the fact that you're asking, means you need more help than I originally thought."

"Okay, yes. Damn it. We've been together, more than once. That's all you need to know. And I think she had feelings for me."

"Had?"

"I blew it with her."

"Yeah, well, going behind her back to search for a nanny might do that."

"I explained the reason I did that."

"To me, but you never told Mia your reasons."

"I never had the chance. I wanted her to calm down so I could explain it rationally to her, but then I made that slip about her family and I was forced to tell her I'd had her investigated."

"The final nail in the coffin."

Adam nodded and admitted quietly, "I did it for Rose."

"I believe you, but you're going to have a hard time convincing Mia about your intentions, because you won't open yourself up. She's been telling you all along that's what she wants. Why are you holding back? It's obvious you're crazy about her."

"It is?"

"Aren't you?"

Adam gave it some thought. "With Rose came Mia. I think of them as one. I guess I never realized it before. They were a package deal almost from the beginning."

"You adore Rose. *And Mia.* They are a gift. All tied up into a bow for you. So what are you afraid of, Adam?"

Adam rubbed his temples again. The pain in his head pounded with the truth. He'd been plagued by guilt and uncertainty for years, safeguarding his heart so securely, that he'd kept himself away from serious relationships and love. He'd hidden behind his work and his need for privacy. "Mia was right. I've been closed off a long time. I don't know how to let anyone in."

"You let me in, Adam. Of course it took Mom's health episode to accomplish that, but I think you're ready to let Mia in. If she wasn't important to you, you wouldn't have called me. And don't give me that business that you were worried about how to get Rose home without hurting Mia in the process. If you want Rose back, all you have to do is go get her. You have legal rights to her, Adam. But you want more than that. And I'm telling you, don't wait until it's too late. The clock is ticking. Go after what you want right now. Tell Mia how you feel. And hurry the hell up."

"I hate it that you're right," Adam said, finishing his drink.

"And I hate it that you've got a gorgeous woman and child waiting for you." Brandon smiled. "I've had to live knowing you'd saved my life and there was no damn way for me to reciprocate. At least now I feel I may have helped save yours."

Adam smiled back. "That makes us even."

"Get your child and woman back first. Then we'll be even."

The front porch swing moaned as Mia rocked Rose in her arms. The quiet sound lulled the baby to sleep. This house had been her home once, when Grandma Tess had taken all of them in, and now she was back, feeling that same sense of loss, the hurt blistering her up inside. Her grandmother was a rock, a solid, rational, wise woman and Mia needed to be here with her now. She needed the comfort Grandma Tess provided. She always knew the right thing to say. Mia was wounded. She'd begun to trust again. She'd believed in Adam Chase. She'd let go her fears and put her faith in the power of her intense feelings for Adam. He'd sure had her fooled.

Initially she and Adam had spoken about her nanny duties and taking it day by day with no real end in sight. Now that the time had come, Mia couldn't face leaving Rose in the hands of another...a stranger. No matter what had happened between her and Adam, Mia was prepared to forgive and forget in order to live under Adam's roof and care for her niece, if he allowed it.

If that meant swallowing her pride, she would do it. She'd return to Moonlight Beach and keep out of Adam's life the best she could. If she didn't do that, what kind of life would Rose have? She'd have every material thing she might want—Adam's wealth could provide that—but what about love? What if Adam couldn't open himself up to loving his own daughter? What if he held back with her, the same way he'd held back with Mia?

She peered at the slumbering angel in her arms. "Sweet Cheeks, your auntie Mia will not abandon you," she whispered. "Don't worry."

Mia was almost lulled to sleep, too. Gentle breezes reaching this far inland soothed her tired bones until the humming roar of an engine coming down the street reached her ears. She opened her eyes and leaned forward in the swing, watching a Rolls-Royce park in front of the house. The gorgeous car stuck out on this middle-class street, like a diamond among mere stones.

Adam climbed out of the car, and their eyes met. She wasn't surprised to see him. She knew he wouldn't let Rose out of his sight for long, but they'd agreed that he'd call before coming over. Of course, Adam hadn't abided by that rule.

As he wound around the car and approached, a bouquet of lavender roses in his hand caught her attention. Did he think flowers would solve anything? He reached the porch and set one foot on the first step. "Hello, Mia."

She gasped inside, her heart racing like crazy.

"Adam."

He glanced at Rose, love beaming in his eyes. "How long has she been sleeping?"

"Only a few minutes."

"Is your grandma Tess home?"

"Yes."

"I would like to meet her."

"Now?"

"Yes, right now. It's about time I met her. Don't get up. Let the baby sleep. I'll knock and see if she comes to the door."

He walked past her and gave three light raps to the door.

Adam was full of surprises today. Of course Grandma Tess came to the door, and she graciously greeted Adam, bleeder of her heart, and let him inside.

"What on earth?" Mia muttered.

Rose stirred restlessly, stretching out her arms, and Mia pushed off with her bare feet to start the swing swaying again while she strained to listen to the quiet conversation going on in the house.

She sighed. She couldn't hear a thing.

A short time later, Adam walked out the door, minus the flowers. "Mind if I sit with you?"

She shrugged and he sat down. "I like your grandmother, Mia. She's a nice lady."

They spoke softly to keep from waking the baby.

"You were supposed to call to let me know you were coming."

"I didn't want to chance you telling me no."

Adam pushed a hand through his hair. He breathed deeply and turned to face her. "I've missed you, Mia."

"You miss Rose."

"I miss both of you." His eyes narrowed as if he was choosing his words carefully. "You know what I saw when I pulled up to the house just now? I saw my family. You and Rose and me, we're a family. And it doesn't scare me anymore to think it, to say it or to feel it."

"Don't, Adam. You don't have to pretend. I've already decided for Rose's sake I'll come back to Moonlight Beach."

Adam's eyes gleamed and he smiled. "Oh, so you've decided that you can tolerate me. You're making the ultimate sacrifice for the baby by being in my presence."

Had he gone crazy since she'd left him? "Why are you smiling?"

"Because you are so full of it, Mia." What *did* Grandma Tess say to him?

"I beg your pardon?"

"You are. And if you just listen to me for one minute, I'll explain about the nanny."

"Don't forget about the investigation. I'd love to hear your excuse for that one."

"Fine. I'll tell you everything. I hope that'll make up for hurting you. Because, sweetheart, the very last thing in the world I want to do is hurt you again."

He was getting to her. His body nestled next to hers, the tone of his voice and the sincere way he spoke only added to her slow melt. "Start from the beginning, Adam. Leave nothing out."

As Adam spoke about Lily, his little sister who'd looked up to him, who'd followed him around like a lost puppy, who'd trusted him like no other, Mia bit her lip to keep tears from spilling down her cheeks. His voice broke a few times, recounting that horrible day when the tornado ripped through his town and took Lily with it. He spoke of grief and guilt and heartache. About his relationship with his mother and his brother, about how he'd shouldered the blame and let that come between him and his family. He spoke about Brandon, too, and how they'd finally patched up their differences and about how he'd asked Brandon for advice today, needing his brother now more than he ever had before.

Mia was seeing a side of Adam that he'd never revealed. She could relate to the pain they'd endured as a family, the loss, the heartache. "I'm glad you told me."

"I want there to be no secrets between us, Mia." He put his arm on the back of the porch swing and even though he wasn't touching her, his presence surrounded her and she felt safe and protected.

"About the nanny," he said. "It was just a thought to make your life easier. I've seen how hard you work. You come home looking tired and drained at times. I know how much Rose means to you, and you do it without complaint. But you hold down a full-time position, take care of Rose and your grandmother and have to put up with me. It's a lot of responsibility. The nanny idea came to me, only as a means to provide you with some backup. Believe me, I was going to run it by you, but then we started getting closer and I didn't want to ruin what we had going. Being with you two in Texas was wonderful. I've never been happier, and I did tell you that."

"You did," Mia admitted.

"And then Mom got sick and we had to rush home. The

whole thing slipped my mind. Mia," he said, his arm wrapping around her shoulder. "No one could replace you." The depth of his voice had her believing him.

A tear trickled down her cheek. "Thanks."

He went on, "Do you remember how we met?"

"Of course, I cut my foot and bled all over you."

Adam chuckled. "Not quite. But you came to Moonlight Beach to find out what you could about me, right? Why did you do that?"

"I've already told you. I couldn't just turn Rose over to a stranger. I needed to find out what kind of person you were."

"Exactly. I regret having you investigated now, but weeks ago when all I knew about you were the lies you'd told me, I needed to know the same thing. You were going to live under my roof and help me raise my daughter. What I did wasn't too different than what you did. We just had different ways of going about it. We were both trying to protect this little girl." He pointed to Rose, love shining in his eyes. "Because she's precious to both of us."

"Adam, the difference is I would've answered all of your questions truthfully. You, on the other hand, went out of your way to evade mine."

"True. That was the old Adam. I don't like to talk about myself."

"You really mean you don't like letting people know you."

"You know me now, Mia. You know everything about me. And I'm happy about it. Loving you has changed me."

Hot tingles rose up from her belly. "What did you just say?"

Adam grinned. "I love you, Mia. At first I thought my feelings were just for Rose, but Brandon, of all people, helped me see what was right in front of me. I'm in love with you, Mia. You and Rose own my heart."

"We do?"

"Yes, you do."

Adam leaned over and brushed his lips over hers. She'd never known a sweeter kiss. "Oh, Adam." Tears spilled down her cheeks freely now. She could hardly believe this was happening. She moved closer to him on the porch swing, and his next kiss wasn't sweet at all, but soul-searching and magical.

"I love you, Adam Chase. I tried really hard not to."

"I'll take that as a compliment, sweetheart, and thank God you love me. Must've been my mad first aid skills."

A chuckle burst from her lips. "That was it. That's why I love you so much I can hardly stand it." The baby fussed, a little sound of displeasure. "Adam, I think the baby wants her daddy."

"I'll take her," Adam said, and she transferred Rose into his arms. Adam cuddled her close and turned to face Mia. "Before she wakes up and howls, I have a question for you." A hopeful glint entered his eyes.

"What is it?"

"I've asked for your grandmother's blessing and she's given it to me."

Mia took a big swallow at the reverent tone in his voice.

"I've never asked this of another woman. Will you come home to Moonlight Beach and be my wife? You, me and our little Rose, we're already a family, but I want to make it official because I love both of you with all my heart. I'm asking you to marry me, Mia."

Mia touched his arm and gazed into his beautiful eyes. She no longer had to hold back her love for him; she let it flow naturally, and it was liberating and wonderful. "Yes, Adam. I'll marry you."

"We'll have a good life, Mia. I promise. I want to take you to Italy. We'll honeymoon there, the three of us."

"It's always been a dream of mine."

"I know, sweetheart. I want to make your dreams come true."

Their gazes locked, and warmth seeped into her heart. She loved this man like crazy. He would be a wonderful father and an attentive, loving husband. She had no doubt.

"Uh-oh," Adam said. "Looks like little sleepyhead is waking up. Do you want her back?"

"No, you hold her, sweetheart."

"Okay, but she's not going to like this."

Rose's eyes opened, she fidgeted and took a glance around. Her lips parted and they waited for her complaint.

"Coo, coo." Precious sounds reached their ears.

She gurgled a few times, and then her chubby hand reached up to touch Adam's face.

His brows lifted, creasing his forehead. "Would you look at that."

"I'm looking," she said, awed. Her little Rose had perfect timing.

The baby peered at her daddy's handsome face. Her mouth opened and spread wide, revealing a gummy toothless beautiful smile.

Adam's eyes welled up. "I think I've won her over, Mia."

"Adam Chase, only you can win two female hearts in one day."

"Our sweet little matchmaker helped make that happen."

"She's brilliant, just like her daddy."

Adam kissed her then, and Mia's heart swelled. Their baby Rose did have a way about her. She was going to wrap them both around her finger.

And there was no place either of them would rather be.

* * * * *

Adam's story is not only a
BILLIONAIRES AND BABIES *novel,*
but is also part of the
MOONLIGHT BEACH BACHELORS *trilogy*
by USA TODAY *bestselling author Charlene Sands*

Pick up the first book in this series
HER FORBIDDEN COWBOY

Available now from Harlequin Desire!

And don't miss the next
BILLIONAIRES AND BABIES *story*
DEMANDING HIS BROTHER'S HEIRS
from USA TODAY *bestselling author Michelle Celmer*
Available August 2015!

If you're on Twitter, tell us what you think of
Harlequin Desire! #harlequindesire

#2389 DEMANDING HIS BROTHER'S HEIRS
Billionaires and Babies • by Michelle Celmer
Holly never knew her late husband had an identical twin until the man showed up on her doorstep, demanding to help raise *her* twin sons. Will the secret he keeps stop him from winning her heart?

#2390 HAVING HER BOSS'S BABY
Pregnant by the Boss • by Maureen Child
Brady Finn's mission is to take his company to the next level. Aine Donovan plans to stop him. But soon their searing attraction gets the better of them, leading to a pregnancy shocker nobody expected!

#2391 THE PRINCESS AND THE PLAYER
Dynasties: The Montoros • by Kat Cantrell
As a member of Alma's recently reinstated royal family, Bella Montoro must marry for the sake of her country. The only hitch: she's falling for her fiancé's black sheep brother...

#2392 SECOND CHANCE WITH THE BILLIONAIRE
The Kavanaghs of Silver Glen • by Janice Maynard
Once, all Ellie Porter wanted was Conor Kavanagh, but a decade later, this single mom needs him for one thing only—to save her brother. As old passion rekindles, will Conor save her, too?

#2393 A ROYAL BABY SURPRISE
The Sherdana Royals • by Cat Schield
When college professor Brooke Davis falls for the mysterious Nic Alessandro, little does she know he's actually the prince of a small European country and their romance is about to leave her with an heir to the throne!

#2394 THAT NIGHT WITH THE CEO
by Karen Booth
PR expert Melanie Costello has signed on to make over millionaire Adam Langford's rebellious image—even though the CEO is her former one-night stand. Surely she can resist his charms this time. Her career depends on it!

REQUEST YOUR FREE BOOKS!
2 FREE NOVELS PLUS 2 FREE GIFTS!

H HARLEQUIN®

Desire

ALWAYS POWERFUL, PASSIONATE AND PROVOCATIVE

YES! Please send me 2 FREE Harlequin® Desire novels and my 2 FREE gifts (gifts are worth about $10). After receiving them, if I don't wish to receive any more books, I can return the shipping statement marked "cancel." If I don't cancel, I will receive 6 brand-new novels every month and be billed just $4.55 per book in the U.S. or $5.24 per book in Canada. That's a savings of at least 13% off the cover price! It's quite a bargain! Shipping and handling is just 50¢ per book in the U.S. and 75¢ per book in Canada.* I understand that accepting the 2 free books and gifts places me under no obligation to buy anything. I can always return a shipment and cancel at any time. Even if I never buy another book, the two free books and gifts are mine to keep forever.

225/326 HDN GH2P

Name _____ (PLEASE PRINT)

Address _____ Apt. #

City _____ State/Prov. _____ Zip/Postal Code

Signature (if under 18, a parent or guardian must sign)

Mail to the **Reader Service:**
IN U.S.A.: P.O. Box 1867, Buffalo, NY 14240-1867
IN CANADA: P.O. Box 609, Fort Erie, Ontario L2A 5X3

Want to try two free books from another line?
Call 1-800-873-8635 or visit www.ReaderService.com.

* Terms and prices subject to change without notice. Prices do not include applicable taxes. Sales tax applicable in N.Y. Canadian residents will be charged applicable taxes. Offer not valid in Quebec. This offer is limited to one order per household. Not valid for current subscribers to Harlequin Desire books. All orders subject to credit approval. Credit or debit balances in a customer's account(s) may be offset by any other outstanding balance owed by or to the customer. Please allow 4 to 6 weeks for delivery. Offer available while quantities last.

Your Privacy—The Reader Service is committed to protecting your privacy. Our Privacy Policy is available online at www.ReaderService.com or upon request from the Reader Service.

We make a portion of our mailing list available to reputable third parties that offer products we believe may interest you. If you prefer that we not exchange your name with third parties, or if you wish to clarify or modify your communication preferences, please visit us at www.ReaderService.com/consumerschoice or write to us at Reader Service Preference Service, P.O. Box 9062, Buffalo, NY 14240-9062. Include your complete name and address.

HD15

SPECIAL EXCERPT FROM

HARLEQUIN

Desire

Brady Finn's mission is to take his company to the
next level. Aine Donovan plans to stop him. But when
searing attraction leads to a pregnancy shocker, they'll
both need to reevaluate just what it is they want from
each other...

Read on for a sneak peek at *HAVING HER BOSS'S BABY*,
the first in **Maureen Child**'s
PREGNANT BY THE BOSS trilogy!

The door opened and there she was. He'd been prepared
for a spinsterish female, a librarian type.

This woman was a surprise.

She wore black pants and a crimson blouse with a
short black jacket over it. Her thick dark red hair fell
in heavy waves around her shoulders. She was tall and
curvy enough to make a man's mouth water. Her green
eyes, not hidden behind the glasses she'd worn in her
photo, were artfully enhanced and shone like sunlight in a
forest. And the steady, even stare she sent Brady told him
that she also had strength. Nothing hotter than a gorgeous
woman with a strong sense of self. Unexpectedly, he felt
a punch of desire that hit him harder than anything he'd
ever experienced before.

"Brady Finn?"

"That's right. Ms. Donovan?" He stood up and
waited as she crossed the room to him, her right hand
outstretched. She moved with a slow, easy grace that
made him think of silk sheets, moonlit nights and the soft
slide of skin against skin. Damn.

"It's Aine, please."

"How was your flight?" He wanted to steer the conversation into the banal so his mind would have nothing else to torment him with.

"Lovely, thanks," she said shortly and lifted her chin a notch. "Is that what we're to talk about, then? My flight? My hotel? I wonder that you care what I think. Perhaps we could speak, instead, about the fact that twice now you've not showed the slightest interest in keeping your appointments with me."

Brady sat back, surprised at her nerve. Not many employees would risk making their new boss angry. "Twice?"

"You sent a car for me at the airport and again at the hotel. I wonder why a man who takes the trouble to fly his hotel manager halfway around the world can't be bothered to cross the street to meet her in person."

When Brady had seen her photo, he'd thought *efficient, cool, dispassionate*. Now he had to revise those thoughts entirely. There was fire here, sparking in her eyes and practically humming in the air around her.

Damned if he didn't like it.

It was more than simple desire he felt now—there was respect, as well. Which meant he was in more trouble here than he would have thought.

Need to find out just how this business venture goes?
Don't miss HAVING HER BOSS'S BABY
by USA TODAY bestselling author Maureen Child

Available August 2015

www.Harlequin.com

THE WORLD IS BETTER WITH

Romance

Harlequin has everything from contemporary, passionate and heartwarming to suspenseful and inspirational stories.

Whatever your mood, we have a romance just for you!